As you probably guessed from the picture, Atticus closely resembles me! I mean me, Henry the cat, not me, Jennifer Gray, the author. I'm thrilled to have so many fans and wanted to let you know that my, I mean, Atticus's new adventures are even funnier and more exciting than the last one. Thanks Jennifer for turning me into an action-cat hero! And thanks, you guys, for reading.

Henry (and Jennifer)

Praise for Atticus

'Atticus is the coolest cat in the world. This is the coolest book in the world.'
Lexi, age 7

'Atticus Claw is fantastic because it has interesting creatures and characters. I especially like Atticus.'
Charlotte, aged 8

'I think that this book is the best book I've ever read because it's so funny!'
Yasmin, age 10

'Fun and exciting, Atticus Grammiticus Cattypuss Claw is the most cutest. Once i opened it i just couldn't put it down.'
Saamia, age 9

'It's mysterious – it makes you want to read on.'
Evie, aged 7

'I would recommend it to a friend.'
Mollie, aged 10

'Once you start to read it you can't stop!'
Molly, age 8

ATTICUS CLAW
Settles a Score

Jennifer Gray is a barrister, so she knows how to spot a cat burglar when she sees one, especially when he's a large tabby with a chewed ear and a handkerchief round his neck that says Atticus Claw. Jennifer's other books include *Guinea Pigs Online*, a comedy series co-written with Amanda Swift and published by Quercus. Jennifer lives in London and Scotland with her husband and four children, and, of course, Henry, a friendly but enigmatic cat.

By the same author

ATTICUS CLAW
Settles a Score

ATTICUS CLAW
Breaks the Law

ff

faber and faber

First published in 2012
by Faber and Faber Limited
Bloomsbury House, 74–77 Great Russell Street,
London WC1B 3DA

Printed in England by CPI Group (UK) Ltd, Croydon, CR0 4YY

A CIP record for this book
is available from the British Library

ISBN 978–0–571–28449–8

Atticus Grammaticus Cattypuss Claw – the world's greatest cat burglar – was lying on a comfy bed in Monte Carlo when a messenger pigeon landed on the window ledge. Atticus opened one eye, then the other. Finally, with a yawn, he stretched lazily, jumped off the bed and padded over towards the window.

'Are you Claw?' The messenger pigeon said cautiously.

'Who's asking?' Atticus replied, examining his sharp talons.

'Never you mind.' The pigeon shivered. He blinked at Atticus. He had been told to deliver the note to a brown-and-black-striped tabby with a chewed ear, four white socks and a red handkerchief with its name embroidered on it tied round its neck. He was sure he'd got the right cat. It looked a nasty piece of work; but then most cats did as far as he was concerned. 'I've got a message for you.'

'Hand it over then,' Atticus purred, jumping on to a table and holding out a paw.

'No chance!' the pigeon sidled away from him along the ledge. Carefully, watching Atticus all the time with his beady eyes, he unclipped the tube containing the message from his leg and threw it on the table.

Atticus flipped off the lid, reached in with a claw and uncurled a tiny piece of paper. He stared at the message. It was in a strange scratchy writing he didn't recognise.

To: Atticus Grammaticus
Cattypuss Claw

We have a job for you. Meet us on Tuesday. Littleton-on-Sea. 11.15. At the pier. Don't be late.

Come alone. Or else.

PS: It will be worth your while.

'Who gave you this?' Atticus demanded.

The pigeon looked frightened. 'I can't remember,' he cooed.

Suddenly Atticus pounced. His left paw pinned the pigeon's tail. 'Don't waste my time,' he hissed. 'I want to know who gave you this.'

The pigeon looked more frightened than ever. 'I can't say,' he squawked. 'They'll kill me if I do. And worse! You're not supposed to find out until you get there. Help! I'm in a tizzy!' The pigeon fainted.

Atticus let go. 'Hmmm,' he said, reading the message again. 'Interesting . . .' He glanced at the dazed bird. Pigeons always talked. Yet this one had kept its beak shut. Whoever had sent the message, Atticus decided, had certainly scared the poo out of the pigeon.

For a moment he hesitated, wondering what to do. Then he grinned. All cats like mysteries – that's why they're called 'curious'. And Atticus was no exception. In fact Atticus *loved* a mystery. Especially when he was at the centre of it.

The pigeon came to with a start. 'Well?' he trembled. 'What shall I tell them?'

'I'll be there,' Atticus said.

The pigeon looked relieved.

'Off you go, then.' With a sweep of his paw, Atticus pushed the startled bird off the ledge.

He watched it flap away. Then he padded down the stairs and went into the study. The computer was on. He tapped out the words *Littleton-on-Sea* expertly with his claws. A picture of a sleepy cobbled town next to a flat grey sea popped up on the screen. It didn't look much, Atticus thought. Not exactly the sort of place you'd expect a summer crime wave. But he could soon change that! Tapping away at the keyboard, it didn't take him long to work out exactly how he was going to get there. Then, without a backward glance, he slipped out of the cat flap, jumped on a train to the nearest port and boarded the next cruise ship to England.

At about the same time that Atticus Claw was talking to the messenger pigeon in Monte Carlo, three
black-and-white birds with dark blue wings and jade-
green tails flew down from the sky and landed by the
side of the main road leading to Littleton-on-Sea.
They were magpies.

They crowded round the limp body of a fourth
bird, nudging it with their claws. The first magpie
had a tuft of grass in its beak. The second one had a
twig. The third hopped from one foot to the other,
dipping his head and dangling a worm.

None of the birds spoke. The only sound was of
the occasional car rushing by.

After a little while the first bird, the glossiest and
sleekest of the three, with cruel glittering eyes to
match, dropped his offering of grass beside the dead

bird's tail. He nodded to the others. 'You can begin the funeral now, Slasher,' he cawed quietly.

The second magpie, who was thin and scrawny with a hooked foot, hopped forwards and arranged the twig neatly beside the tuft of grass. 'Huh hum.' He cleared his throat and bowed his head. 'We are gathered here together,' he began, 'in the sight of the A1234, to say farewell to our dear friend, Beaky.'

The third magpie, who was fatter than the other two and had feathers missing from his tail, let out a sob.

'It's all right, Thug,' the first magpie put a consoling wing around his friend's heaving body. 'It's good to cry.'

'Beaky was truly one of us,' Slasher continued. 'He was mean and horrible and nasty. Everyone hated him. He helped give magpies the bad name we're so proud of. He stole eggs and scared baby birds. He woke people up at five o'clock in the morning with his awful voice—'

'—Chaka-chaka-chaka-chaka . . .' Thug managed a throaty chuckle between sobs.

'He loved bashing blackbirds and chasing chickens—' Slasher's voice was breaking. He wiped tears away with the black tip of his wing. 'He was an example to us all. I'm sure I squawk for everyone when I say I'm going to miss him.' He hopped aside to make way for the first magpie. 'Now Jimmy will say a few words.'

'Thank you, Slasher; that was beautiful.' Jimmy Magpie preened his glossy feathers. His eyes glittered like diamonds. Looking down at the roadside, he addressed the dead bird in a solemn voice. 'You were our friend, Beaky – a valued member of the gang. We lived together, we fought together and we stole together.' He paused. 'Good times!' He let out a cry. 'Chaka-chaka-chaka-chaka-chaka.' It was harsher than Thug's – more of a battle cry. Then his voice hardened. 'Yours is the third funeral I've been to this year, Beaky. First Goon. Then Penguin. Now you. All squished by the side of the road. All mangled by murderers. All crushed by *cars*.' Suddenly he looked up sharply. 'Any more clues yet, Slasher? You were with him when he died.'

Slasher shifted uncomfortably. 'I'm sorry, Boss. All I know is that it was a Rolls-Royce. I didn't get the number plate. It all happened so fast.'

Jimmy Magpie glared at him menacingly before turning back to his task. 'As I was saying . . . Goon, Penguin and Beaky. All flattened like pancakes by our sworn enemy . . . *humans*.' Jimmy Magpie spat the word out.

Slasher and Thug nodded. They had heard the speech before. At Goon's funeral. And Penguin's.

'But this time the death won't go unavenged,' Jimmy Magpie continued, his beak set. 'This time, we magpies are going to fight back.'

Thug and Slasher looked at one another, puzzled. This bit was new.

'What are we gonna do, Boss?' Slasher flexed his wings. 'I mean, I don't mind having a go at one but you've got to admit them humans are an awful lot bigger than us.'

'They may be bigger,' hissed Jimmy Magpie, 'but most of them are stupid.'

'Let's scare baby birds.' Thug's beak was twitching with excitement. 'Humans hate that!'

'That's hardly original, Thug, and it's the wrong time of year.' Jimmy Magpie sounded bored. 'Baby birds are born in spring. This is the summer, in case you haven't noticed.'

'What about waking them up at five o'clock in the morning with our beautiful singing?' Slasher suggested.

'*You* can if you want, Slasher,' Jimmy Magpie shook his head impatiently, 'but I've got something much more evil in mind.'

'What? Like raiding a chicken coop for eggs?' Thug chuckled. 'Good thinking, Boss. That always gets them going.'

'Still too small, Thug,' Jimmy Magpie said. 'Think bigger. Think *outside* the nesting box.'

'You mean, like get some help?' The words were out of Slasher's beak before he realised Jimmy might get mad.

'CHAKA-CHAKA-CHAKA-CHAKA-CHAKA!' Jimmy Magpie's voice rose in his harsh chatter. He flew up and beat the air furiously with his magnificent wings.

Slasher hid behind what was left of Beaky. 'I didn't mean it, Jimmy. Honest I didn't,' he trembled. 'Everyone knows you're the boss.'

Jimmy Magpie put his head to one side and gazed at Slasher without blinking.

'Sorry, Jimmy!' Slasher hopped his scrawny frame behind Thug for protection. 'Please don't peck me!'

'*Peck* you, Slasher?' Jimmy said smoothly. 'I wouldn't do that. In fact, you're absolutely right,' he crowed. 'We *could* use a little help. Which is why I've

11

already made contact with someone I've heard of; an animal almost as fiendish as me, who's perfect for what I've got in mind.'

'No way, Boss.' Thug gaped at him. 'No one's as fiendish as you!'

'Thank you, Thug.' Jimmy Magpie preened.

'Who is he, Boss?' the magpies chattered.

'Tell us!'

'Yeah, please tell us!'

'His name,' Jimmy Magpie said slowly, 'is Atticus Grammaticus Cattypuss Claw . . . he's the world's greatest cat burglar and he's going to steal every piece of jewellery in Littleton-on-Sea.' He paused. 'For us.'

'A cat . . .' gasped Thug.

'Burgling humans . . . ?' cawed Slasher.

'For magpies.' Jimmy Magpie watched it sink in. 'Exactly.' A nasty smile was spreading across his beak. 'And the beauty of it is that even if the cat gets caught, no one will ever suspect in a million years that he's working for us.'

'It's brilliant, Boss!' Thug and Slasher said together, looking at their leader in awe.

'I know,' Jimmy Magpie said modestly. He straightened up. 'Now that's enough chattering. We've got work to do. You two start checking out the best houses to burgle.'

They nodded.

'And I'll get down to the pier and prepare for the cat.'

Then the three magpies spread their wings and took off up into the blue sky.

At number 2 Blossom Crescent, Littleton-on-Sea, the Cheddar family was sitting down to breakfast. At least the children – Michael, who was eight, and Callie, who had just turned six – were sitting down. Mrs Cheddar and her husband, who had recently been appointed as the town's Police Inspector, were rushing round in circles looking for his badge.

'I had it yesterday,' Inspector Cheddar shouted. 'I put it down on the kitchen table ready to polish it in the morning and now it's disappeared!'

'It can't have, darling,' Mrs Cheddar said mildly, opening cupboards and looking inside. 'Have you checked the fridge?'

'I didn't put it in the fridge!' Inspector Cheddar yelled. 'It's a police badge, not a pint of milk!'

'Can't you go without it, just this once?' Mrs

Cheddar suggested. She was already running late for work.

'No!' Inspector Cheddar wailed. 'The Chief Inspector of Bigsworth is coming to the station today. I need to make a good impression if I'm ever going to get a job at Scotland Yard.' (Getting a job at Scotland Yard was Inspector Cheddar's lifelong ambition.) 'If he sees me without my badge he'll put me on traffic duty.'

'Perhaps Mrs Tucker knows where it is,' Mrs Cheddar said, rummaging inside the pan drawer. 'She'll be here any minute.'

Mrs Tucker was the Cheddars' childminder. She came in the mornings and afternoons to help with breakfast and tea and to take the children to and from school while Inspector and Mrs Cheddar were at work.

At the mention of Mrs Tucker, Michael and Callie grinned at one another. They liked Mrs Tucker. She

was fun. *And* she was on their side in what had become known as 'The Battle of the Pet'.

The Battle of the Pet had started when the Cheddar family moved house for Inspector Cheddar's new job. Inspector Cheddar had promised the children they could have a pet to help them get used to their new home. Mrs Cheddar had agreed. Now they were both too busy with work to do anything about it. But Michael and Callie hadn't given up hope; especially as Mrs Tucker was on the case.

They heard the roar of a motorbike pulling up. A key turned in the latch. A few seconds later Mrs Tucker strode in.

'Sorry I'm late,' she said, taking off her helmet and patting down her frizzy grey hair. She thumped her basket on the table. 'I had to help Mr Tucker mend his nets.' She winked at the children as she pulled off her leather jacket and stepped out of her biker boots. 'Just in case he meets one of those horrible *you-know-whats* when he's out in his boat today.' She reached in her basket for a pair of slippers and an apron.

Michael and Callie giggled. Mr Tucker was a fisherman. The children had never met him, but he sounded awesome. A horrible *you-know-what* was a sea monster. According to Mrs Tucker, Mr Tucker regularly came across them when he was out catching sardines.

'Not to worry, Mrs Tucker,' Mrs Cheddar said cheerfully. She pulled her head out of the washing machine. 'Only we've lost Inspector Cheddar's badge. You don't know where it is, do you? He needs to polish it.'

'It's in the fridge,' Mrs Tucker said at once, as if it were the most obvious thing in the world. 'I saw it lying about last night and thought to myself, he'll be looking for that in the morning so I'd better put it in a safe place.'

'I told you!' Mrs Cheddar exclaimed.

The children giggled.

'How stupid of me,' Inspector Cheddar said sarcastically. He opened the fridge and plucked his badge from the vegetable drawer. 'I should have known it was here all along.'

Mrs Tucker ignored him. 'Now if you had a *dog*,' she looked meaningfully at the children, 'you could train it to find things for you.'

'No!' Inspector Cheddar said firmly.

'Please, Dad!' Callie cried.

'Yeah, Dad,' Michael joined in. 'You promised we could have a pet.'

'I'm too busy to look after a dog,' Inspector Cheddar said irritably, getting the Brasso out from under the sink. 'So's Mum.'

'What about a cat?' Mrs Tucker suggested. 'They're easy to take care of. They don't need walking, for a start.'

'I love cats!' Callie cried.

'Well, I *hate* them,' Inspector Cheddar declared, rubbing away at the badge with a duster. 'They're nasty scheming things with no sense of loyalty. Like criminals.'

'Nonsense!' Mrs Tucker declared. 'Mr Tucker had a cat once which was cleverer than a human. It used to help him navigate. It saved his life in a storm more than once.'

'I very much doubt it,' Inspector Cheddar said rudely. He didn't believe any of Mrs Tucker's stories about her husband. He put his badge down on the window ledge and opened the window to get rid of the smell of Brasso. He didn't want the Chief Inspector of Bigsworth to suspect he'd polished it in a hurry.

'Go on, Mum,' Michael begged. 'Please can we have a cat? Callie and me will look after it, I promise.'

'Well . . .' Mrs Cheddar hesitated. She'd been going to say 'yes' (she liked cats too) but decided she'd better not upset her husband any more. 'It's really up to Dad.'

'And Dad says NO,' Inspector Cheddar said again.

Michael and Callie looked disappointed.

'Never mind,' Mrs Tucker whispered loudly. 'We'll get round him one way or another.'

'I heard that, Mrs Tucker.' Inspector Cheddar sat down next to the children and poured himself a mug of tea. 'And I'd like to remind you, I am a Police Inspector. No one "gets round" me.'

There was an awkward silence.

'CHAKA-CHAKA-CHAKA-CHAKA!!'

Everyone looked up in surprise. Two magpies had landed on the window ledge. They didn't seem remotely frightened of the humans. In fact, they hardly seemed to have noticed the Cheddar family at all. They were staring at something else.

'Quick, Dad!' Michael cried. 'They're after your badge!'

The thinner of the two birds hopped towards the newly polished badge and opened its beak.

'Over my dead body!' Inspector Cheddar sprung out of his chair and ran to the sink. 'Shoo!'

he shouted, flapping his hands at the birds. 'Shoo!'

The two birds hopped along the windowsill, but they didn't fly away.

'Nasty things, magpies,' Mrs Tucker muttered, shaking her head.

'Why?' asked Callie.

'They're just birds,' said Michael. 'Aren't they?'

'They're not *just* birds,' Mrs Tucker said in a hushed voice, as though she didn't want the magpies to overhear her. 'They steal things. And you should never cross them.' She shivered. 'It's like breaking a mirror. Magpies bring bad luck.'

'Now then, Mrs Tucker.' Inspector Cheddar turned his back on the magpies. 'None of your superstitious old wives' tales, please. Michael's right – they're just birds.' He started to pin his badge to the top of his sleeve. 'OUCH!'

'What's the matter now?' Mrs Cheddar asked anxiously.

'I just stuck the pin in my arm!' Inspector Cheddar moaned. 'What a morning!' He grabbed his cap and left.

'I told you magpies bring bad luck,' Mrs Tucker said darkly. 'How's it going up at Toffly Hall, dear?' she asked, changing the subject.

Mrs Cheddar was helping to organise an antiques fair to be held in the grounds of a nearby stately home. The fair was going to be filmed for the TV show *Get Rich Quick!*

'All right, I suppose,' Mrs Cheddar sighed. 'But it's only ten days away and there's still so much to do. We're expecting hundreds of people to bring things to be valued. I just hope it all goes smoothly.' (Mrs Cheddar was also secretly hoping that if it *did* go smoothly then Rupert Rich, the presenter, might offer her a job on the programme.)

'*Attack the attic, make a packet!*' Mrs Tucker roared. (That was Rupert Rich's famous catchphrase.)

'Can we come?' asked Michael excitedly.

'Of course you can,' Mrs Cheddar said. 'You'll love it. There's going to be a real mixture of stuff. Lots of trash, probably – there always is – but some really beautiful things as well; people will bring jewellery and watches – and of course there's Lady Toffly's tiara.'

'What's a tiara?' Callie asked.

'It's a sort of hairband,' Mrs Cheddar smiled, 'made of diamonds.'

'It sounds wonderful,' Mrs Tucker sighed. 'I wish I had something like that tucked away in the roof.'

'You should have a look,' Mrs Cheddar said. 'You never know what might be there.'

'*Attack the attic, make a packet!*' Michael and Callie shouted.

'Huh!' Mrs Tucker snorted. 'All I'm likely to find is a load of Mr Tucker's old fish hooks. Now come along, you two,' she told the children, 'let's get you off to school.' She went to get their bags while Mrs Cheddar kissed them goodbye and set off to work.

When their mum had left, Michael and Callie got down from the table and went to wash their hands. The magpies were still at the window. They gazed at the children with black beady eyes.

'Chaka-chaka-chaka-chaka!' cawed one.

'Chaka-chaka-chaka-chaka!' the other cackled.

Callie frowned. 'It sounds like they're laughing at us,' she whispered.

'I know what you mean,' Michael said. He studied the birds carefully. One was thin and scrawny with a hooked foot, the other was fat with feathers missing from its tail. The birds stared back at him. 'It's as if they've been listening to our conversation!' Michael shivered. For some reason the two birds gave him the creeps. Maybe Mrs Tucker was right – maybe they *did* bring bad luck.

'If we had a cat, it could chase them away.' Callie grinned.

'Yeah, like *that's* going to happen! You heard what Dad said, Callie – he *hates* cats. We'll be lucky if we get a goldfish.' Michael leaned over the sink as far as he could and pulled the window shut.

4

Two days later, Atticus Grammaticus Cattypuss Claw purred goodbye to the old lady in whose wheelie basket he'd been riding and stepped off the bus in Littleton-on-Sea. The journey had been reasonably straightforward: a comfortable cabin on a cruise ship with a couple from Spain who thought he was the ship's cat and brought him delicious scraps every mealtime; followed by a pleasant train journey in first class and a short ride on the bus with the old lady in a shopping basket full of biscuits. He rubbed the crumbs off his whiskers. *So far*, he thought, *so good*.

Atticus looked about him, taking in his surroundings. To his left was a parade of open-fronted shops and cafés, which wound its way into the distance. The shops sold ice cream and buckets and spades and postcards. The delicious smell of fish and chips wafted from the cafés. Atticus sniffed the air. *Maybe later*, he thought, turning his back. Right now, he had business to attend to.

Across the road was the sea. The tide was out and the beach seemed to stretch for miles, flat and muddy-looking. Only a few people were on it. Atticus could understand why. A cold wind was blowing and it had started to drizzle. Like all cats, one of the things Atticus disliked most was rain. Fluffing out his coat, Atticus sighed. He missed Monte Carlo already.

Sidestepping a little girl with sticky hands who wanted to stroke him, Atticus crossed over to the beach, hunching his shoulders against the wind, and jumped on to the sea wall. From here he had a better view of the pier. It stood a little way along the sand, beside the car park. He gazed at it, taking in every detail. It was roughly as wide as railway tracks and stuck out into the sea for about a hundred metres. Rusty rails ran along both sides of the wooden walk-way, which was held up by huge iron pillars covered in seaweed.

Atticus approached cautiously along the wall, ready to disappear in an instant if there was any trouble. He reached the car park and gazed along the walkway. The pier was deserted. There was no sign of anyone. Or anything. Atticus hesitated. He heard the town clock strike once to signal the quarter hour. 11.15. He was bang on time. But where was the mysterious client who had sent for him?

Suddenly he heard a strange noise.

'*CHAKA-CHAKA-CHAKA-CHAKA!*'

The chattering was loud and angry as though someone or something was warning him off. He listened again. The sound was coming from somewhere *below* the pier, where the iron columns held the walkway in place. Atticus jumped down lightly on to the sand and tiptoed under the pier. He followed it out towards the sea, glancing up from time to time. About halfway along, he stopped. Balanced between several rusty struts way above him was a scruffy mess of twigs and leaves. Leaning over the side of it were three bright-eyed birds with black heads and flashes of blue and white on their wings.

'*Magpies!*' he whispered.

'What are you doing down there?' the first of them jeered.

'Yeah, if you're Claw and you're really as good as you say you are, you'll climb up here so we can talk,' the second one sneered.

The third one said nothing, but even from a distance and in the shadow of the pier, Atticus could see its eyes glittering.

Atticus thought about walking away. He'd never worked for a bird before. People: often; dogs: sometimes; cats: occasionally; and once a pig who paid him to steal every truffle in Italy – but never a bird! A cat working for a magpie? The idea was ridiculous. And yet . . . Atticus's curiosity got the better of him again. *What on earth could a bunch of magpies want with him?* He couldn't resist staying long enough to find out. And if they *were* just messing around, he decided, he could always give them a nasty fright and go and get some fish and chips.

'Sure,' he agreed lazily, jumping on to one slippery beam and then to the next, balancing effortlessly on the thin edges.

Soon, he reached the ledge where the magpies perched. They had climbed out of the nest to greet him. 'Well,' said Atticus, sitting down and popping out his claws one by one. 'Here I am.' He smiled, making sure the birds could see just how sharp and white his teeth were. 'Now, what do you want?'

When they saw his fangs, the two magpies who had shouted down at Atticus when he was a safe distance below – a fat one with ragged tail feathers, and a thin one with a hooked foot – dropped their beaks to their chests and fluttered backwards, away from him. But the other one – who Atticus took to be the boss – stood his ground and looked him straight in the eye.

'It's very simple,' Jimmy Magpie said quietly. 'We want you to steal all the jewels in Littleton-on-Sea and bring them here to us.'

Slasher nodded. Thug chattered to himself.

Atticus raised a whiskery eyebrow. He'd heard people say that magpies were thieves, but he'd never suspected they could be *this* greedy. *What do they want with all that loot?* he wondered. Most thieves fenced jewels for cash. A few kept the most treasured items for their own use in necklaces (or collars if they were cats or dogs). *But this lot?* They couldn't use cash and, as far as Atticus knew, birds didn't do bling.

'Suppose I agree,' he said eventually, when the

bird didn't elaborate. 'I prefer to go in through cat flaps and open windows. I can't guarantee I'll clean the whole town out.'

'I see . . .' Jimmy Magpie blinked at Atticus coldly. 'Well I think you'll find my boys can help you get into most places if you can't manage it.'

'I don't want their help,' Atticus snapped angrily. 'I'm the best cat burglar in the world, remember?'

There was a tense silence. 'Very well,' Jimmy Magpie said finally. 'We'll do it your way. We find the houses. You hit them.'

'What's in it for me?' Atticus demanded. He didn't like the way the magpie did business. Nobody spoke to Atticus Grammaticus Cattypuss Claw like that: least of all a bullying bird. He'd almost decided to leave on the next boat.

'Sardines,' Jimmy Magpie said, watching Atticus carefully. 'Four per hit.'

Atticus wavered. *Sardines!* His mouth watered at the thought. He couldn't resist sardines. 'Eight,' he countered.

'Six,' the magpie snapped back.

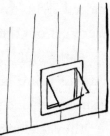

'Done.' Sardines were sardines. Whatever doubts Atticus

might have had about taking the job he decided to put to one side, for the time being at least. 'I'll start tonight.' He got up to go. 'By the way,' he asked as an afterthought, 'how did you hear about me?'

'We magpies keep our eyes and ears open.' Jimmy Magpie shrugged. He looked sharply at Atticus. 'We're *everywhere*. And we know *everything*. So don't try and double-cross us.'

Suddenly Atticus remembered the messenger pigeon. Now he understood why it hadn't talked. Jimmy and his gang must have terrified it.

'You don't frighten me . . .' Atticus hissed. 'And you'd better be careful what you say, or the deal's off.' He drew himself up and arched his back. 'I'll have you three for lunch before you can say "feathers".'

The two other magpies were trembling, but Jimmy showed no sign of fear. Instead he grinned and held out a claw. 'No need for that, my friend!' he cawed slyly. 'We're partners now! Come on, boys. Let's get out the sardines and celebrate.'

Thug and Slasher hopped back into the nest. Atticus heard heaving and panting as they flipped a fish over the edge.

'I'll eat alone, thanks,' Atticus said, catching the

sardine in his teeth and making his
way back down to the beach.

'Suit yourself,' Jimmy Magpie
called after him. 'Make sure
you're back here tonight at midnight.'

There was no reply. Atticus had gone.

'Why didn't you tell him about the antiques fair at
Toffly Hall, Boss?' Slasher asked, peering down.

'Yeah, that lady in Blossom Crescent said there'd
be loads of jewellery there,' Thug reminded him.

'And watches,' Slasher said eagerly. 'Isn't that why
we hired the cat? To steal things for us?'

'You keep your beaks shut about that for now,'
Jimmy hissed.

'Why, Boss?' Thug's face was puzzled. 'I thought
the cat was gonna help us.'

'Help himself more like,' Jimmy said. 'I'm not
sure I trust Atticus Claw . . . yet. It didn't take him
long to threaten us, did it?' Jimmy dipped his head
angrily. 'Typical cat. He thinks he can call all the
shots. Doesn't want to be told what to do by a bird.'

'We could try and burgle the houses ourselves,'
Slasher suggested.

'Yeah,' Thug agreed. 'Tell Claw we don't need him.'

31

Jimmy shook his head impatiently. 'We can't break safes. We don't know how to open cupboards. And we make too much noise – or you two do, anyway.'

Thug and Slasher looked sheepish.

'We need a pro,' Jimmy continued. 'Which means, for the time being at least, we need the cat.' His eyes gleamed. 'So let's keep the antiques fair a secret until we know more about him. See if he delivers on the burglaries or if he tries to double-cross us. In the meantime, you two get up to Toffly Hall and case the joint.'

Once he'd finished his sardine and had a quick snooze, Atticus felt better. So what if Jimmy Magpie and his gang were a bunch of bullies? It wasn't his problem. You couldn't be choosy about who you worked for or you'd never get paid. He would do the job, take the sardines and scram like he always did.

But first, he needed to find somewhere to live.

Atticus had chosen a sheltered spot beside an empty beach hut to eat his sardine. Now he turned away from the sea and retraced his steps past the pier and back to the shops. He paused in front of a shiny metal ice-cream stand and gazed at his reflection. He lifted a paw and adjusted the handkerchief around his neck so that his name was clearly visible. He heard the clock strike two. Ten hours to go until he started thieving. There was plenty of time for him to find a comfy bed, have another snooze and get some more grub. Satisfied with his appearance, Atticus wandered in the direction of town in search of his next temporary human.

At half-past three, Mrs Tucker was waiting for Michael and Callie at the school gates.

'I thought you might like a snack.' She ripped open two packets of crisps as they started the short walk home to Blossom Crescent.

'What's for tea?' Michael asked. The crisps seemed to be making him even hungrier. 'I'm starving.'

'I've brought you something special,' Mrs Tucker replied

'What?'

'Sardines!'

'Sardines?' Callie pulled a face. 'Yuk!'

'Don't knock 'em,' Mrs Tucker said briskly, 'till you've tried 'em. They're delicious. *And* they're good for your brain.' She tapped her basket. 'Mr Tucker caught them fresh today. In fact they're so fresh they're practically still swimming.'

'Can I see them?' Michael asked, curious. He flipped open the lid of the basket.

'Not till we get home,' Mrs Tucker snapped it shut. 'We don't want every cat in the area following us, do we?'

Callie pulled at Mrs Tucker's sleeve. 'That one already is,' she said. 'Look!' She pointed to a large brown-and-black tabby with four white socks and a red handkerchief tied around its neck. It was walking a few paces behind them.

Mrs Tucker stopped and looked at the cat.

The cat stopped and looked at her.

'I wonder what happened to its ear,' she remarked, before walking on again. 'It's all chewed.'

Michael glanced back. 'It's still following us,' he said.

'It's not following *us*,' Mrs Tucker corrected. 'It's following the sardines. And you're not having any,' she said, turning round suddenly and glaring at the cat. 'They're for the children's tea.'

The cat regarded her steadily. 'Meow,' it said.

'Can we stroke him?' Callie asked. 'He's so cute.'

Mrs Tucker hesitated. 'I suppose so,' she said. 'Mind he doesn't scratch though.'

The children approached the cat cautiously.

Michael held out a hand and scratched him gently under his chin. Callie stroked his fur. The cat began to purr. He arched his back with pleasure.

'I think he likes us,' Michael said.

Mrs Tucker snorted. 'I think he likes our sardines!' she muttered.

'I wonder what his name is,' Callie said.

Michael felt round the cat's neck under the handkerchief. 'He doesn't have a collar.'

'But look! There's some writing on this,' Callie noticed, bending down and examining the corner of the handkerchief carefully.

The cat didn't move. He lifted his chin.

Michael knelt down beside his sister. He peered at the tiny embroidered letters. They were as delicate as a spider's web. 'Att-i-cus . . . Gramm-a-t-i-cus . . . Catt-y-puss . . . Claw,' he read slowly. 'Do you think *that*'s his name?'

The cat purred loudly.

'It's awfully long.' Mrs Tucker frowned. 'For a cat. Mr Tucker just called his one Bones.'

'I like it,' said Callie. 'It rhymes. Apart from Claw, that is.'

'He seems to recognise it, anyway,' Michael said, rubbing the cat's ears. 'Don't you, Atticus?'

The cat's purring became a low throaty roar – like a car engine

when you first switch it on.

Michael turned the handkerchief over. 'There's no phone number.' He tried to keep the excitement out of his voice. 'Do you . . . er . . . think he belongs to anyone?' he asked casually.

'I know what you're thinking, Michael Cheddar,' Mrs Tucker said firmly, 'but you can't keep him.'

'Why not?' Michael asked, disappointed. 'I thought you *liked* cats.'

'I do,' Mrs Tucker said.

'And you *want* us to *have* a pet.' Callie reminded her. 'You said so this morning.'

'I know I did. But just because he doesn't have a collar doesn't mean he doesn't belong to anyone,' Mrs Tucker explained. 'Especially with a name like that.'

'He might not, though,' Michael insisted. 'He might be a stray.'

'Someone must have tied that hanky round his neck,' Mrs Tucker told him. 'I mean, he didn't just put it on himself, did he?'

'He might have,' Callie said.

'Cats are clever,' Michael added. 'You said so this morning.'

'Never mind what I said this morning!' Mrs Tucker

puffed out her cheeks. 'The point is it wouldn't be fair for us to take him if he's already got a home. Think how his poor owner would feel. I mean, what if he was *your* cat and someone lured him away with a basket of fish?'

'But what if he's lost?' Michael insisted. 'Shouldn't we at least look after him for a bit and try and find out who his owner is?'

The cat had sat down while the argument was in progress. Now he stood up again and rubbed his body against the children's ankles, purring gently.

'See!' Callie cried. 'That's what he wants!'

'Well . . .' Mrs Tucker hesitated. 'He does look a bit lost.' She thought for a moment. 'I'll tell you what. If he's still following us when we get back to the house, we'll take him in and see if we can find out where he's come from. If he isn't, that's the end of it. OK?'

'OK,' the children agreed.

'No peeking to see if he's still there until we get to the front door,' Mrs Tucker added. 'And pretend to ignore him or he'll think it's a game.' She marched off.

The children gave the cat a final stroke and followed reluctantly.

The rest of the walk was agony. Michael and Callie plodded along in silence, eyes to the ground. Even Mrs Tucker telling them about the time Mr Tucker beat off a giant lobster with his wooden leg couldn't distract them.

Eventually, after what seemed an age, they reached number 2 Blossom Crescent. Michael opened the gate. He and Callie raced up the path to the front door. 'Well?' said Michael. He heard the gate click shut and screwed his eyes together. He couldn't bear to look. 'Is he still there?'

Callie covered her eyes with her hands.

There was a pause. The children held their breath. They heard Mrs Tucker mutter, 'I thought as much!' They crossed their fingers.

'All right, you two,' Mrs Tucker said, 'you can look now.'

The children opened their eyes. The cat was sitting on the pavement a few feet away peering at them through the gate.

'Meow?' he said.

Callie gave a shriek of delight and started jumping up and down.

Michael grinned.

Even Mrs Tucker chuckled. She eyed the cat for a

moment. Then she opened the basket. A strong fishy smell wafted out. The cat's good ear pricked up. He lifted his chin and sniffed the air. 'Well, what are you waiting for, Atticus Grammaticus Cattypuss Claw?' Mrs Tucker said, reaching for her keys. 'You'd better come in.'

'But what will Dad say?' Callie looked worried all of a sudden. 'Do you think he'll be cross if he comes home and finds Atticus?'

'I don't expect he'll be very pleased,' Mrs Tucker said. 'But Atticus won't be staying for long. Only till we find out who he belongs to.'

'And it's not like we went out and bought a pet when Dad told us not to,' Michael added.

Callie's face brightened. 'It's more like Atticus found *us* because he needs someone to look after him for a little while!' she cried.

'Exactly,' Mrs Tucker agreed. She opened the door. 'Come on, then, Atticus, make yourself at home.'

'Yes, come on, Atticus,' Michael encouraged.

'Please, Atticus,' Callie begged.

The cat stood up slowly. It yawned and stretched. It looked up and down the street. It looked at the house and the garden. It looked at the cars parked in the road. It looked at Michael, Callie and Mrs Tucker. Finally, it looked at the basket. Then, as if it had come to a decision, it squeezed through the gate and strolled past them into the house, its tail held high in the air.

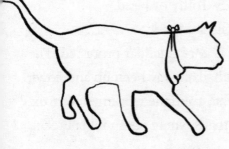

6

Up at Toffly Hall Mrs Cheddar was having problems with Lord and Lady Toffly over the marquee.

'I don't want it there,' Lady Toffly snapped. 'It'll spoil the begonias. They need sunshine. Don't you agree, Roderick?'

'Yes I do, Antonia,' Lord Toffly said gruffly. 'Besides, it interferes with the view from the library.'

'We can't have that!' Lady Toffly cried.

'Ridiculous!' Lord Toffly agreed. 'Some people have no consideration.'

'Take it down!' Lady Toffly ordered.

'At once!' Lord Toffly shouted.

'But, Lady Toffly . . .' Mrs Cheddar protested. The marquee was huge. It had already been up and down three times since breakfast and the workmen were exhausted. 'You agreed that's where we should put it.'

42

'I assure you I didn't, Mrs Cheddar,' Lady Toffly snapped. 'I said the *west* lawn. This is the *east* lawn.' 'Some people can't tell one end of a compass from the other!'

Lord Toffly glared at Mrs Cheddar.

Mrs Cheddar bit her lip and tried to think about nice things, like bunnies and squirrels and little tweetie birds, instead of punching a Toffly on the nose, which is what she wanted to do. 'Lady Toffly,' she said, 'when we put it on the west lawn, you told us to move it to the north lawn. When we put it on the north lawn you told us to move it to the south lawn. When we put it on the south lawn you told us to move it here, to the east lawn.'

'Well, I still don't like it,' Lady Toffly declared. She glared at the workmen who were lying on the grass, panting. 'Tell them to stop sprawling about and move it again.'

'Lazy lumps,' Lord Toffly snorted, sitting back on his shooting stick.

Mrs Cheddar's foot twitched. Just one little kick aimed at Lord Toffly's big fat tweeded bum would send him sprawling into Lady Toffly's precious begonias . . . But then they would fire her and she would never get a job on *Get Rich Quick! Tweetie birds*, she told herself firmly. *Bunnies. Squirrels.* 'Where would you like us to move it to?' she sighed.

Lady Toffly thought for a moment. 'How about the *south-west* lawn,' she suggested.

'Good idea, Antonia,' Lord Toffly agreed.

'And if that doesn't work we can try the *north-east* lawn, and if I don't like that there's the *south-east* lawn and then . . . um . . .'

'Don't forget the *north-west* lawn, Antonia!' Lord Toffly reminded her.

'Of course, Roderick. How brilliant of you.'

'OK,' Mrs Cheddar said wearily, adding *kittens* to her list of nice things to think about. She pointed to a spot away from the begonias. 'Let's try over there.'

'Give me a shout when you've finished.' Lady Toffly gave a little giggle. 'I'm going to try on my tiara. It's worth millions, you know.'

'Billions, my love.' Lord Toffly cracked his knuckles gleefully. 'Trillions probably. *Zillions* even. I wouldn't be surprised.'

'Quite so, Roderick. I doubt whether Rupert Rich will have seen anything like it before!'

'Chaka-chaka-chaka-chaka!'

Thug and Slasher were sitting in a nearby tree, watching.

'I feel a bit sorry for her,' Thug said.

'Which one?' Slasher asked. He was a slightly short-sighted.

'Not the ugly one with the big yellow teeth and knobbly knees,' Thug said, pulling a face. 'The one we saw the other morning at the window in Blossom Crescent. She seems nice.'

'*Nice*?' Slasher squawked, ruffling his feathers. '*Nice*? She's a human. All humans are horrible. They're magpie murderers. Jimmy says so.'

'I know, but . . .'

'Remember what happened to Beaky?' Slasher said sharply.

'Yeah, but . . .'

'And Goon?'

'Yeah . . .'

'And Penguin?'

'*She* didn't kill them though,' Thug pointed out.

'She might have,' Slasher said. 'How do *you* know? And anyway it doesn't matter. They're all humans. And all humans are horrible.' He gave Thug a quick peck. 'Keep your mind on the job.'

45

'All right, Slasher, don't get your feathers in a twist!' Thug retorted, hopping backwards.

'I can't wait to tell the boss how much the tiara's worth,' Slasher said. He chuckled softly. 'Those toffee-nosed Tofflys will be *really* mad when we steal it.'

'D'you think we can get a look at it before we go?' Thug asked wistfully. 'I haven't seen *anything* glittery all day.' He eyed the house. Toffly Hall was enormous. The two magpies had spent the day looking in almost every window for a glimpse of treasure, without much success. For rich people, Thug thought, the Tofflys didn't seem to have many shiny things – just a lot of dusty old books and shabby furniture.

'Yeah, why not?' Slasher agreed. 'It makes sense to check it out properly before we nick it at the fair.' He grinned at Thug. 'The bedrooms are round the front. Let's take the short cut. Come on.'

They flew over the roof and landed on a window ledge.

'Look, there she is.' Slasher peered into the dark room.

'It's on her head!' Thug cried. He gazed in delight.

Lady Toffly was dancing around the room in a tartan dressing gown, holding a small mirror; the tiara perched on her head. The magpies stared at it with longing.

'It's all sparkly,' Thug sighed.

'And spangly,' Slasher giggled.

'It's lovely!' They gave each other a hug.

'SHOOO!'

Suddenly the window flew open.

'Get away, you horrible things!' Lady Toffly shrieked, flapping at them with a slipper. 'Roderick! Quick! Get your shotgun!'

'Chaka-chaka-chaka-chaka!'

The birds fell off the ledge.

'Shotgun!' Slasher yelped.

'I can't afford to lose any more feathers,' Thug cried. 'I'll crash!'

'Where is he?' Slasher looked about wildly.

'I dunno!' Thug flapped to and fro. 'Let's hide before he pots us!'

They fluttered down to the gravel and scuttered into the hedge.

'RODERICK! Where are you?' Lady Toffly leaned out of the window. 'Hurry up!'

'I'll be there in a minute, Antonia.' Lord Toffly's voice came from the other side of the hedge.

'What are you doing?' Lady Toffly screeched.

'I'm cleaning the Rolls-Royce,' Lord Toffly replied. 'There seem to be some feathers stuck in the bumper.'

Thug and Slasher looked at one another. Their beaks dropped open.

'Did he say Rolls-Royce?' Thug whispered.

Slasher nodded.

'And feathers?'

Slasher nodded again.

'You don't think . . . ?'

'Shhhhh!'

Lord Toffly's footsteps crunched across the gravel. The front door slammed shut.

Slasher peered out from under the hedge. 'Quick! Follow me.'

The magpies emerged from their hiding place and hopped over to the Rolls-Royce.

'Is that the car?' Thug asked, staring at the powerful machine in awe. 'The one that killed Beaky?'

Slasher pecked viciously at the paint. 'That's the one, all right. Look!'

A little heap of black and white feathers lay on the gravel beside the bumper.

'Beaky!' Thug whispered. He started to sob.

'Don't get all soppy, you big idiot,' Slasher warned.

His beak was set grimly. 'And DON'T go around saying humans are nice. EVER AGAIN.' He took one last look at the feathers, which started to blow away in the breeze. 'Come on, Thug,' he said. 'Let's go and tell Jimmy.'

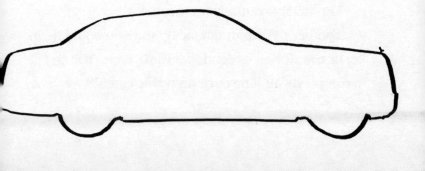

Inspector Cheddar was in a good mood. The meeting with the Chief Inspector of Bigsworth had gone surprisingly well. The Chief Inspector had been very friendly. He had even commented about how shiny Inspector Cheddar's badge was. Better still, he had given him a Very Important Job to do.

'I want you to be in charge of security at the Toffly Hall antiques fair,' the Chief Inspector said. 'There will be lots of valuable things on display, including the Tofflys' tiara. The eyes of the world will be on Littleton-on-Sea. We don't want to take any risks. Do you understand, Cheddar?'

'Yes, sir. You can rely on me, sir!'

'You get this right, Cheddar, and you could be in for a promotion – Scotland Yard, even. You get it wrong and you'll be back on traffic cones.'

Inspector Cheddar had no intention of getting it wrong. Organising the security at the Toffly Hall antiques fair was exactly the sort of job he'd been trained for. No sneaky, low-life crook was going to get past him and his officers. He would see to that.

Inspector Cheddar arrived home at six o'clock. He opened the front door quietly. He was a little earlier than usual and he wanted to surprise the children. He tiptoed into the hall, closed the door gently behind him and hung his jacket up on the coat stand. Then he stood for a moment, listening.

To his surprise, the house was silent.

Inspector Cheddar frowned. He'd been expecting to hear shrieks of laughter coming from upstairs and the sound of splashing water. The children normally had tea at five and then a bath, one after the other, at six. *That's strange*, he thought. *Where is everyone?* Mrs Tucker was normally a stickler for routine.

He made his way through to the kitchen. *Phew!* It stank of fish. Sardines, if he wasn't very much mistaken. *What a pong!* He'd never been very keen on sardines.

Holding his nose with one hand, Inspector Cheddar took off his cap with the other, threw it on the table and hurried to open the back door.

51

To his horror, it was unlocked.

Inspector Cheddar was furious. Wasn't he *always* telling Mrs Tucker not to leave the doors and windows unlocked when she went out? Anybody could walk in off the street! Why, if this were the city they wouldn't have a stick of furniture left!

Muttering to himself, he went to fill the kettle. A pile of dirty dishes was stacked in the sink. Inspector Cheddar stared at them. *What was going on?* Mrs Tucker *never* left dirty dishes in the sink. Anxiously, he checked the fridge. Apart from a pint of milk, some eggs and a few potatoes, it was empty. Inspector Cheddar's eyebrows shot up. *Something was definitely wrong.* Mrs Tucker *always* left supper for him and Mrs Cheddar in case they were late home from work.

He gulped. An awful thought had occurred to him. *Something must have happened to Michael or Callie.*

Inspector Cheddar rushed to the table and snatched up his cap.

It was then he saw the note, lying beneath it. He held it up.

Dear Inspector Cheddar,

Don't worry if we're not here when
you get home. The children are fine.
They have a surprise for you. We
just had to pop out for a bit of
shopping.

See you soon,
Mrs Tucker

PS Mrs Cheddar phoned to say she'll
be late back from Toffly Hall because
the marquee keeps moving.

Inspector Cheddar let out a sigh of relief. He read the note again. *A surprise!* He loved surprises. What adorable children he had. Callie was so sweet; Michael was so thoughtful. And Mrs Tucker – she might leave back doors unlocked and talk a lot of nonsense about navigating cats and battles with sea monsters but her heart was in the right place. He began to regret losing his temper at breakfast. Perhaps a pet wouldn't be *so* bad as long as it wasn't anything too big.

He thought for a moment. He didn't want anything *furry*. Mice gave him the creeps. So did rats. Rabbits scratched the furniture and there was something about guinea pigs and hamsters he didn't trust. *What then?* Suddenly he had a brainwave. Goldfish! They were friendly and fun. And they only cost 50 pence! Inspector Cheddar rubbed his hands happily. He couldn't wait to tell Michael and Callie when they got home. They'd be thrilled. He would take them to the pet shop at the weekend and let them choose their very own goldfish.

Pleased with his decision, Inspector Cheddar decided to get changed. He went back into the hall and put one foot on the stair. Then he froze.

THWUMP! A sound came from

somewhere upstairs. Inspector Cheddar swallowed. His hands started to shake. *A burglar!* Inspector Cheddar's good mood evaporated. He went purple, then white. It was just as he feared. The burglar must have sneaked in the back door and gone upstairs when everyone was out.

He thought fast. What he should really do was phone the station and ask for help. On the other hand, burglars didn't often appear in Littleton-on-Sea (never, actually, since he had arrived) and this was his Big Chance to catch one red-handed. Inspector Cheddar took a deep breath. *Blow the station!* He would handle this himself. He still had the advantage. The burglar didn't know he was there. He'd been as quiet as a mouse when he came in because he wanted to surprise the children. Well, it wasn't the children who were in for a surprise. It was the sneaky snoop snaffling through his sock drawer searching for swag who was going to get it in the snout. Inspector Cheddar grabbed an umbrella from the coat stand and crept up the stairs.

At the top he paused. A strange noise was coming from the main bedroom – a sort of low rumbling, like a car engine. What on earth was it? Inspector Cheddar listened carefully. He pushed open the door slowly. The noise stopped.

'I know you're in there,' Inspector Cheddar said loudly.

Silence.

'Come out with your hands up.'

Silence.

'Don't make me come in and get you.'

Silence.

'I'm an Officer of the Law.'

Silence.

Inspector Cheddar swallowed. This was harder than he'd thought it would be. 'All right.' He raised the umbrella. 'You've asked for it.'

The Inspector rushed into the bedroom, tripped over Atticus, who was on his way out, and banged his head on the end of the bed.

'You might have told me!' Inspector Cheddar sat on the sofa holding a bag of frozen peas to his forehead.

Mrs Cheddar had just got back. 'I didn't know!' she protested. 'And anyway, the children said they'd left him in their bedroom with the door shut. They just popped out to get him some cat food. You weren't supposed to find out about him until they got home.'

'You gave the poor animal a nasty fright!' Mrs

Tucker scolded. 'Sneaking about like that.'

'I gave *him* a nasty fright!' Inspector Cheddar repeated incredulously. 'What about me?!'

Mrs Tucker scowled. 'He probably thought you were a burglar. He's terrified. The children can't get him down from the top of the cupboard.'

'The question is what are we going to do with him?' Mrs Cheddar interrupted anxiously.

'Well, he can't stay here,' Inspector Cheddar said firmly.

'But, darling,' Mrs Cheddar exclaimed, 'you can't just turn the poor animal out. He's lost!'

'And he's had a fright,' Mrs Tucker said. 'He'll get run over. Then what will the children say?' She glared at Inspector Cheddar. 'They don't forget things, children. Like elephants, they are. They'll probably never forgive you.'

Just then Callie came rushing into the living room clutching a bag of treats. It was half empty. 'We got him down!' she cried.

'Here he is!' Michael followed immediately behind Callie. He was carrying Atticus in his arms. Atticus was purring throatily.

'Oh, aren't you lovely!' Mrs Cheddar sprang up and started petting him.

'I'll get his basket!' Mrs Tucker rushed off to the kitchen. 'He needs a lie-down after a shock like that.'

'But he's been lying down all afternoon!' Inspector Cheddar protested. 'On *my* bed!'

'*Our* bed, darling,' Mrs Cheddar corrected him gently.

'He *can* stay, right, Dad?' Michael asked. 'At least until we find out who he belongs to?'

'I really don't . . .' Inspector Cheddar began.

'I think he should,' Mrs Cheddar interrupted firmly. 'At least for tonight.'

Atticus lifted his head wearily. He gazed at Inspector Cheddar with mournful green eyes.

'I still say . . .' Inspector Cheddar tried again.

'Look at him, poor little lamb!' Mrs Tucker returned with the basket. 'I'd hate to think of him out there all alone! Anything might happen.'

'But . . .'

'Please, Dad?' Callie begged. 'Just for one night?'

Inspector Cheddar knew when he was beaten. 'Oh, all right then,' he said heavily. 'Just for one night.'

8

Later, at eleven-thirty precisely, Atticus woke up in the kitchen. The alarm on Mrs Cheddar's mobile phone (the same phone which he had carefully removed from her handbag while she was brushing her teeth) was buzzing urgently. He reached out a paw and switched it off. The magpies were expecting him at the stroke of midnight. He had to get down to the beach.

But first of all he had to get out of the house.

Atticus had noted with grudging approval how carefully Inspector Cheddar had locked and bolted the front and back doors before he went to bed. Even Atticus Grammaticus Cattypus Claw, the world's greatest cat burglar, might struggle to open them. He was glad he didn't have to. He'd just pretend he wanted to go to the loo outside instead. In fact he'd make such a nuisance of himself the Cheddars would have to get a cat flap installed. Then he could come and go as he pleased until the time came in a week or so for him to leave for good.

He got out of his basket and padded up the stairs. Outside the children's room he paused, wondering whether to wake one of them up to let him out.

Usually Atticus stayed away from kids. They had sticky hands, made too much noise and pulled his tail. He'd only followed them that afternoon because the sardines were calling to him from Mrs Tucker's basket.

He'd been a bit put out when the three of them shut him in a bedroom to go shopping but it had been easy enough to stand on his hind legs and twist the knob to let himself out.

He'd been even more put out when Inspector Cheddar started creeping around the house pretending to be a burglar, especially when he'd tripped over Atticus just when Atticus was coming out to say hello.

It had also come as a nasty shock that Inspector Cheddar was a policeman.

But everyone else had been very nice. They had cuddled him and given him treats and told Inspector Cheddar off for scaring him.

Atticus reckoned he'd fallen on his feet. It wasn't often you got two sardines in one day, let alone half a bag of treats as well. And where better to hide from the law than right under its nose? Besides, he decided, he quite liked Callie and Michael. It might even be fun to hang out with them when he wasn't stealing things.

He nudged the door open with his nose.

Callie's bed was by the door. She'd fallen asleep clutching something soft and squashy in her arms. Atticus jumped up to take a closer look. It looked like a cat. Not a real one, but a pretend one made out of white fluffy material with plastic threads for whiskers and glass beads for eyes. Atticus had seen similar things in shop windows. They were called 'toys'. He'd always wondered what they were for.

He jumped down. Michael's bed was beneath the window. A piece of paper and some crayons lay beside it. Atticus walked over. He stared at the drawing. Two large green-crayoned eyes stared back at him out of a round brown-striped face, a bright-red handkerchief coloured in beneath it. Besides the eyes, the face boasted a tiny pink nose, a grinning mouth with neat white teeth and long white whiskers. It was topped off with a triangle on one side and a bump on the other. Atticus was startled. Was that supposed to be *him*? He didn't think his ear was *that* chewed. He put up a paw and felt it gingerly. No, definitely not. Carefully, he took the brown crayon in his mouth and re-drew the ear so that it looked more like the other one. *That's better*, he thought, sitting back and feeling proud of his work.

It seemed a shame to wake the children after all, so he wandered across the landing into the Cheddars' room and leapt on to the bed.

Neither Inspector Cheddar nor Mrs Cheddar woke up.

Atticus regarded them curiously. Inspector Cheddar was sprawled out, clutching a silver badge of some sort in his fist. A bag of soggy peas lay beside him on the pillow. He was snoring. Mrs Cheddar lay curled up, her sleeping face twisted into a frown. Suddenly her foot jerked out from under the duvet. '*Rabbits*,' she sighed. '*Squirrels*.' She began to smile. '*Tweetie birds*.'

Atticus's good ear twitched. The adult Cheddars were very strange people, he decided. He'd never met anyone like them before.

He told himself to concentrate. He didn't want to be late for Jimmy and his gang. Meowing pitifully, he poked Inspector Cheddar firmly in the eye with his front paw.

'You took your time.' Jimmy Magpie was waiting for Atticus on the sand.

Thug and Slasher stood nearby, watching carefully.

'We thought you'd changed your mind.'

'Chaka-chaka-chaka-chaka.' Thug and Slasher hopped closer.

'I'm here, aren't I?' Atticus snapped. He hated the sound the magpies made. It was almost as if they were laughing at him.

Jimmy regarded him thoughtfully. 'Better late than never,' he said sarcastically. 'I *suppose*. Slasher – get the bag.'

'Yes, Boss.' Slasher hopped over to a small rock and pulled at something. The rock shifted as he pulled the thing free. It was a white plastic bag, rolled up tightly and tied with string.

'Let's go.'

Slasher gathered the string in his beak and flew off awkwardly, the bag dangling at his throat. Thug followed.

'After you, Atticus,' Jimmy said with mock politeness. 'We don't want you losing your way.'

Atticus walked stiffly. Thug and Slasher circled ahead of him, the white tips of their wings picked out by the moon. He could hear the slow beat of Jimmy's wings behind him. Worse, he could feel Jimmy's eyes boring steadily into him. Those eyes! Atticus had only once known eyes so cruel before. And that was from a time he didn't want to be reminded about, ever again. With a start, he found the fur on the back of his neck standing on end, even though the night air wasn't cold. He forced himself to relax. Jimmy Magpie couldn't harm him. He was just a bird. *Do your job*, Atticus told himself, *and go*. Strangely he almost added the word '*home*', but he stopped himself just in time. He didn't have a home. And he didn't want one. The

 Cheddars were his temporary humans, that was all. DGI, Atticus. It was one of the lessons he'd learnt as a kitten. Don't Get Involved.

He put all thoughts of 2 Blossom Crescent out of his mind and padded on.

After a few minutes, he saw a large bungalow nestling in a cul-de-sac on the other side of the road from the sea front, somewhere behind the beach hut where he had eaten his sardine when he first arrived.

Thug and Slasher flew down to the garden and landed on the grass.

'Well?' Atticus slipped through the gate to join them. He tried to sound business-like. 'What have we got?'

'A Mr and Mrs Pearson.' Jimmy glided down beside him. 'Thug, can you fill us in?'

'Yeah, they're loaded,' Thug said. 'The safe's in the bedroom – in the wardrobe. We've seen them taking things in and out. Glittery things,' he added slyly.

'Which section of the wardrobe?' Atticus asked.

'Middle. There's a shelf. Above where she keeps her knickers.' Thug grinned rudely.

'How do I get in?' Atticus glanced at the front door. It was made of thick glass. 'Is there a cat flap round the back?'

'No. But they always sleep with the window up. They've got them locks that stop it opening more

66

than four inches.' Thug chuckled. 'They don't think anyone can get in. Chaka-chaka-chaka-chaka.'

'Well, I can,' said Atticus grimly. 'Anyone else in the house?'

'Nope. Just the two of them.'

'Any pets?'

Thug shook his head.

'Good work, Thug.' Jimmy Magpie stretched a wing and patted Thug on the head. He eyed Atticus. 'We thought we'd give you an easy one to start with,' he said. 'Think you can manage it?'

'Of course I can manage it,' Atticus growled angrily.

He paced round to the back of the bungalow. The bedroom window was open by four inches, just as Thug had said. Atticus leapt up on to the outside ledge. Then he crouched, flattening his shoulders into his body, and wriggled through the gap. He paused for a moment on the inside, opened the curtains cautiously with one paw, and peered into the room.

At one end, to Atticus's left, Mr and Mrs Pearson were asleep in a huge brass bed.

Opposite them, to Atticus's right, a large oak wardrobe stretched the length of the wall.

He jumped down noiselessly and walked to the wardrobe. The doors looked heavy. He would have to use a lever. Whatever happened he mustn't break his claws – he would need them later. Calmly, Atticus looked around for something that would do. A wire coat hanger lay beside a chair. He picked it up in his teeth, the metal scraping uncomfortably against his molars, and dragged it to the wardrobe. Sitting on his haunches he grasped one end between his paws and wriggled the hook into the tiny gap between the two doors. He pulled. Soon there was enough space for him to push in one paw, then a second. Atticus heaved, using his strong hind legs for support. The door opened with a loud creak.

Atticus waited, motionless. There was a snort from the direction of the bed, followed by a series of puffing noises. Then silence.

Atticus jumped on to the shelf above the drawer that held Mrs Pearson's knickers. He was glad to see that the safe was a small one. It nestled at the back of the cupboard, leaving him plenty of room. This one was a key-locking device. Atticus grinned. Humans would call it a piece of cake. *He* called it a piece of steak. He flicked out the claws on his right front paw and got to work.

Seconds later, the safe door swung open. Quickly Atticus untied the handkerchief from around his neck. He spread it out carefully on the shelf. Silently, he emptied the contents of the safe into the centre of the handkerchief – an expensive watch, some gold cuflinks, a pearl necklace and a pair of diamond earrings – piling them up carefully, one on top of the other. Then he took the four corners of the handkerchief and tied them together in a strong knot to make a bag.

Atticus picked it up in his mouth and headed for the window. He jumped on to the ledge and pushed open the curtains.

The magpies were sitting in a line on the other side of the glass. Atticus put the handkerchief down and nudged it under the window with his forehead. Jimmy gave a nod. Thug took hold of the knotted ends in his beak and fluttered clumsily to the ground. Slasher followed. Quickly they unlaced the knot. Two diamond earrings fell on to the grass and glittered in the moonlight.

All at once there was a terrible chattering. 'CHAKA-CHAKA-CHAKA-CHAKA!' It was Thug.

'Shhhhhhh!' Jimmy shut him up with a vicious peck on the head. 'What's the matter with you?' he hissed.

'I'm sorry, Jimmy,' Thug sobbed. 'They're so beautiful. I couldn't help it.'

Suddenly a light went on in the room.

'Stanley?' A woman's voice said. 'Did you hear something?'

It was the Pearsons.

'Quick,' Atticus ordered. 'Get the stuff in the bag.'

Slasher and Thug unrolled the plastic bag and held it open with their beaks. Atticus scooped up the jewels in his paws and threw them into the bag. Jimmy looked on without helping.

'Elspeth?' A man's voice said. 'Did you leave the wardrobe door open?'

'Now scram!' Atticus whispered.

'We've been burgled!' There was a scream from inside the bungalow.

Flapping furiously, Slasher and Thug took off, the bulky plastic bag swaying dangerously between them.

'You get the torch, Elspeth. I'll call the police!'

Jimmy Magpie fluttered up into a tree.

Atticus hesitated. It was too late to make a run for it. Quickly, he hid the handkerchief beneath a bush and pinned himself against the wall.

He heard footsteps. A beam of light fell dangerously close.

'What's that, Stanley?' the woman shrieked.

The beam wobbled as the man took the torch. It flicked over Atticus. Atticus screwed his eyes up tight to shut out the blinding light.

'It's just a cat, Elspeth. That's all.'

The beam moved away.

Once he was sure they weren't looking, Atticus grabbed the handkerchief with his teeth and raced away into the night.

Above him in the sky he heard a faint beat of wings followed by a soft chattering. 'Chaka-chaka-chaka-chaka.' It was Jimmy. This time, Atticus was sure he *was* laughing.

When he neared Blossom Crescent, Atticus began to feel better. He was looking forward to going back to bed.

As he approached the house, to his surprise he saw that the lights were on. Then he saw a car pull away from in front of the gate. It was Inspector Cheddar. Of course! The Pearsons had called the police! Inspector Cheddar would be in charge of the investigation. He was on his way to the scene of the crime.

Atticus wondered what would have happened if Inspector Cheddar had turned up at the bungalow earlier and seen him cowering beneath the window. It wouldn't have mattered, he decided. That was the beauty about being a cat burglar; no human ever suspected you, however suspicious the circumstances. Atticus had been caught red-pawed on several occasions sneaking into people's houses, but they always believed he was after food, not jewellery. The only way he would ever be caught was if someone interrupted him when he was safe breaking or carrying the stuff out in his handkerchief. And that, thought Atticus smugly, would never happen.

He watched the car's tail-lights disappear into the distance, then he slipped through the gate, ran round to the back door and started yowling.

Mrs Cheddar opened the door at once.

'Oh, Atticus!' she cried. 'You're back! We were worried you might have got lost again. We've been out looking for you.'

Atticus felt pleased. He didn't think anyone had ever been out looking for him before. Not at two o'clock in the morning, anyway. He strolled into the kitchen purring.

'Kids!'

Michael and Callie stumbled into the kitchen in their dressing gowns, bleary-eyed.

'Atticus!' cried Michael.

'There you are!' screamed Callie.

Atticus found himself being swept off the floor and into Michael's arms. Callie was tickling his tummy. He wriggled a bit so that she could get her fingers under his armpits.

'I'll bet he's hungry,' Mrs Cheddar said.

'I'll get his food.' Callie rushed to the cupboard and returned with a foil sachet of cat food. She ripped it open. 'Here you are.' She squeezed the gloopy contents into Atticus's shiny new bowl.

Michael set him down gently beside it. 'Go on, Atticus.'

Atticus sniffed at the food. He'd have preferred another sardine, but at least it wasn't that dry stuff that looked like cut-up cardboard and tasted like old dog biscuits. He began to eat.

'What time will Dad be back?' Michael said.

'I don't know,' Mrs Cheddar replied.

'Has there really been a burglary?' Callie whispered.

'Yes, I'm afraid so,' Mrs Cheddar said. 'Somebody broke into a bungalow near the sea and stole some jewellery belonging to some people called Pearson.'

Atticus finished his meal. It was surprisingly tasty – fishy and meaty all at the same time. He stared hard at the shiny dish hoping someone would take the hint and give him some more.

'That's awful!' Callie exclaimed. 'Who would do something horrible like that?'

Atticus's good ear drooped. He looked intently at his empty bowl.

'I don't know, Callie,' Mrs Cheddar sighed. 'There are some nasty people in the world. But I didn't expect to come across them in Littleton-on-Sea.'

Atticus's chewed ear drooped. He kept staring at his bowl. He wasn't hungry any more but he didn't know where else to look.

'Dad's pleased though,' Michael said cheerfully.

'Michael!' Mrs Cheddar gasped.

'I don't mean he's pleased that the Pearsons got burgled,' Michael explained hastily. 'I mean he's pleased there's a crime for him to investigate. He's always complaining that nothing ever happens in Littleton-on-Sea.'

Atticus began to feel better. Michael was right. He shouldn't be feeling guilty. It was a *good* thing he'd stolen the Pearsons' valuables. No wonder Inspector Cheddar was pleased. Policemen liked crime. It gave them something to do.

'Well . . .' said Mrs Cheddar doubtfully.

'If there wasn't any crime, you wouldn't need proper policemen,' Michael pointed out. 'Like Dad.'

'I suppose so . . .'

'And you're always saying how he hates traffic duty.'

'Sort of . . .'

Atticus was beginning to feel quite proud of himself. If it wasn't for him Inspector Cheddar wouldn't have a job! Or if he did, he'd hate it.

Deciding that he *was* still hungry after all, he wandered over to Callie, who was holding the foil packet, and began rubbing at her legs.

'Here you are, Atticus.' Callie squeezed the rest of the food into his bowl.

Atticus ate it noisily. The gravy made it difficult not to slurp.

'Do you think Dad might let us keep Atticus if we can't find his owner?' Callie asked hopefully.

'Let's not worry about that now,' Mrs Cheddar said soothingly. 'Now come on, you two, off to bed.'

She ushered Callie out of the kitchen and flicked off the light.

'Night, Atticus,' Michael said sleepily. He bent down and put his lips to Atticus's chewed ear. 'Promise you'll be nice to Dad,' he whispered, 'so he lets you stay a bit longer.'

I promise, purred Atticus solemnly, settling into his basket as the door closed.

He would commit lots and lots of burglaries so Inspector Cheddar had plenty of crimes to investigate.

That would make him happy. Atticus burped contentedly. *Really and truly*, he thought generously, *it was the least he could do to say thank you.*

One week later . . .

The Chief Inspector of Bigsworth was cross. He had just read the morning paper. There was a picture of him on the front page. Normally the Chief Inspector of Bigsworth would have been pleased by this, but the picture was not a flattering one. It was a photograph of him looking very fat and puzzled, which someone had taken when he wasn't looking. A big caption underneath it read BUNGLING BOBBIES BAFFLED BY BURGLARIES.

The thief had struck again.

'Get Cheddar here,' he shouted to his secretary. 'At once!'

'Yes, Chief Inspector,' she said calmly, picking up the phone. 'There are some people waiting outside to see you.'

'Not more journalists?' The Chief Inspector complained.

'No,' the secretary said. 'Lord and Lady Toffly. They said it was urgent.'

The Chief Inspector groaned. He took out a spotted handkerchief and mopped his brow. The Tofflys! That was all he needed. He had a headache coming on.

Inspector Cheddar arrived at Bigsworth Police Station half an hour later. He was feeling depressed. He'd been at work since seven o'clock that morning, attending the latest crime scene, and he was no closer to finding the culprit of the burglaries than he had been a week ago when they first started.

On his way in he passed two people he recognised – Lord and Lady Toffly.

'It's quite appalling how useless the police are,' Lady Toffly was saying in a very loud voice. 'Don't you agree, Roderick?'

'I do, Antonia. Perfectly pathetic! Especially that hopeless Gorgonzola fellow!'

Inspector Cheddar pulled his cap down over his eyes.

'Cheddar, darling.'

'I don't care what his name is. He's in charge, isn't he? I'd like to take a pop at him with my shotgun.'

Inspector Cheddar hid behind a filing cabinet.

'Roderick!'

'Just to give him a fright, Antonia,' Lord Toffly grumbled. 'I wouldn't *hurt* him.'

Lady Toffly clicked her tongue. 'The point is, Roderick, my tiara is worth *millions* . . .'

'Billions, darling,' Lord Toffly reminded her.

'. . . and the antiques fair is only two days away. What if the thief strikes there? What if he steals the tiara?' Lady Toffly sniffed

'Can't risk that,' Lord Toffly agreed.

'If the police don't catch the culprit soon, we shall have to call it off,' Lady Toffly said. She sighed. 'And after all that trouble we've gone to to set up the marquee.'

'Jolly inconvenient,' snarled Lord Toffly. 'I'd like to give that Gorgonzola fellow a piece of my mind.'

They disappeared.

Inspector Cheddar came out from behind the filing cabinet and made his way to the Chief Inspector's office. He knocked on the door.

'Come in!' a voice yelled.

Inspector Cheddar swallowed. He took off his cap and went into the room.

'Well, what have you got to say for yourself, Cheddar?' The Chief Inspector thundered. He slapped the newspaper down on his desk.

Inspector Cheddar winced when he saw the picture.

'WELL?'

'I'm doing my best, sir,' he quavered.

'YOUR BEST?' roared the Chief Inspector. 'That's clearly not good enough.'

'No, sir.'

'Tell me about the latest break-in,' the Chief Inspector ordered.

Inspector Cheddar drew a notebook from his pocket and consulted it.

'A Miss Rana, sir. Lives at number 17 Sea Shell Drive. Woke to find her safe open and the contents gone. Windows and doors all locked when she went to bed. No sign of forced entry. No fingerprints. Heard and saw nothing.'

'That's it?' the Chief Inspector shouted.

Inspector Cheddar nodded. 'I'm afraid so, sir.'

'No clues?'

'I'm afraid not, sir.'

The Chief Inspector poured himself a glass of water. 'So what you're telling me, Cheddar, is that this thief, whoever he or she is, can walk through walls?'

'Possibly, sir,' Inspector Cheddar said, not wanting to contradict his boss. He had a different theory. He coughed. 'Or come down the chimney.'

'Like Santa Claus, you mean?'

'I suppose so, sir.'

The Chief Inspector banged his glass down on the table. 'Don't be an idiot, Cheddar. Santa Claus isn't a thief.'

'No, sir.'

'And there's no such thing as a burglar who walks through walls.'

'No, sir.'

'You're missing something, Cheddar. That's the problem. Something obvious. You're not behaving like a detective.'

Inspector Cheddar said nothing.

The Chief Inspector of Bigsworth leaned forward menacingly over the desk. 'I want this criminal captured.'

'Yes, sir.'

'The Tofflys want this criminal captured.'

'Yes, sir.'

'The people of Littleton-on-Sea want this criminal captured.'

'Yes, sir.'

'And if you don't arrest whoever it is soon, I'm taking you off the case and putting you back on traffic duty for the rest of your career. Do you understand?'

'But, sir!' Inspector Cheddar choked, 'I don't like . . .'

The Chief Inspector raised his hand to silence him. 'Hard cheese, Cheddar,' he yelled. 'Now get out of here and go and do some proper policing.'

Atticus lay on the sofa waiting for Mrs Tucker and the children to get back from school. He was exhausted. It had been a busy week.

After the near disaster at the Pearsons', things had gone remarkably smoothly. He'd burgled six other houses; two with open windows and four with cat flaps.

Cat flaps might sound easy, especially for a cat burglar, but the problem with them was that sometimes there were actually cats on the other side. If that happened and the cat in question were a lady, Atticus would simply arrange to meet her somewhere and then slip back in when she went out. But if it were a tomcat, that was a different matter. Tomcats defended their territory. Atticus tried to avoid them. He never burgled a house with a dog or a tomcat in it. He touched his chewed ear with his paw and shivered. He didn't want another fight.

This week, though, he'd been lucky. Of the seven houses he'd hit, only one had had a cat in residence: Mimi, a pretty Burmese. Atticus had invited her to meet up at the beach hut, then hidden in the bushes until he saw her go out. He sighed. There were some aspects of the job he didn't like – letting down pretty girls like Mimi was one of them.

Atticus yawned loudly. He was glad he was having a night off. The magpies were having a meeting and he wasn't invited. Atticus didn't care. They could plot and plan all they liked. As long as he got his sardines, he didn't want anything else to do with them. He yawned again. Seven burglaries in as many nights! He hoped Inspector Cheddar appreciated his efforts. Atticus had certainly given him plenty of crimes to investigate.

At that moment Michael and Callie rushed into

84

the room. Atticus rolled on to his back obligingly and dangled his paws in the air. Callie tickled his tummy. Michael rubbed his ears. Atticus purred like a tractor.

Mrs Tucker came in and pushed open the window to let in some fresh air. She regarded Atticus closely. 'That animal's getting fat!' she announced.

Atticus was offended. It was true he'd been eating more sardines than he should – six a day from the magpies and whatever Mrs Tucker brought in her basket from the remains of Mr Tucker's catch – and quite a lot of cat food as well. But FAT! That was just plain rude. Especially coming from Mrs Tucker who looked like she guzzled plenty of sardines herself when no one was looking.

'No, he's not,' Callie said loyally. 'Are you, Atticus?'

Atticus purred in agreement. At least someone was on his side.

'Yes, he is!' Mrs Tucker insisted. 'Look at the size of his tummy. We should put him on a diet.'

Atticus's face fell. Diets meant dusty pellets that looked like mummified rabbit poo. He'd once adopted a matador in Madrid who was obsessed with healthy eating. It had been a bad mistake. Atticus had lost half a kilo in a week.

'Poor Atticus,' Michael laughed. 'Look at his face!'

'He won't be able to get in and out of that cat flap soon,' Mrs Cheddar continued.

The cat flap had been installed, as Atticus predicted, soon after his arrival. Inspector Cheddar had got so cross about being woken up in the middle of the night by Atticus poking his paw in his eye, Mrs Cheddar had ordered it to be put in straight away so that her husband could concentrate on his detective work. Meanwhile Mrs Tucker had asked at the local cats' home if anyone was missing a cat answering to the description of Atticus and had driven round the area on her motorbike looking for 'lost cat' notices. But no one seemed to know anything about a brown-and-black tabby called Atticus Grammaticus Cattypuss Claw. So 'one night' had led to two and two to four and four to . . . well: it looked as though Atticus could be staying a while.

Mrs Tucker was still gazing at Atticus's tummy. 'I wonder if he's being fed by someone else,' she said thoughtfully. 'That's the thing with cats; you never know what they get up to when they're out.' She gave Atticus an accusing stare. 'Especially at night.'

Atticus blushed beneath his fur. *She didn't suspect something, did she?*

'Atticus doesn't do *anything*,' Michael said. 'He's too lazy.'

Atticus raised a whiskery eyebrow. *If only he knew.*

They heard the key turn in the lock.

Mrs Tucker frowned. 'Who's that?' She looked at her watch. 'It's only quarter to four.'

Callie ran to the door. 'It's Dad!' she cried.

Inspector Cheddar came into the room. He threw a newspaper on to the coffee table and sat down heavily beside Atticus.

Mind out! Atticus thought, flicking his tail out of the way just in time.

'Dad!' Michael said. 'You're early.'

'Yes,' said Inspector Cheddar, stroking Atticus absently.

Atticus was startled. Inspector Cheddar had never stroked him before. Normally he ignored him or said things like 'you still here?' or 'get off the bed, you lazy lump'. Atticus began to purr quietly.

'Did you catch the burglar?' Callie asked excitedly.

'No,' Inspector Cheddar shook his head. 'I just came home for a break. It's hopeless. This criminal's a pro. He comes and goes without a trace. He can walk through walls. He can slip through closed windows. He can slide under locked doors. I just don't see how he does it. It's like magic.' He scratched Atticus's ears.

Atticus glowed. It was nice to hear Inspector Cheddar talk about him like that. Maybe he did appreciate him, after all. He purred more loudly.

'I'll never catch him,' Inspector Cheddar commented.

Atticus nodded in agreement. *It was true. He never would.*

Suddenly Inspector Cheddar made a choking sound.

Atticus looked up, astonished. What was the matter now?

'I'm the worst detective in the world!' Inspector Cheddar sobbed. 'I'm awful. Rubbish. A waste of space. I'm rotten, like a mouldy bit of mousetrap.'

Atticus was amazed. Wasn't Inspector Cheddar *happy* he had crimes to investigate?

'No, you're not, Dad!' Michael cried. 'You're the best detective in the world!'

Inspector Cheddar shook his head. 'The Tofflys think I stink. So does the Chief Inspector of Bigsworth,' he howled. 'He's threatened to put me back on traffic duty if I don't catch whoever it is soon!'

Atticus was flabbergasted. This was the first time it had occurred to him that Inspector Cheddar actually expected to *catch* someone for the burglaries, or that he might be upset if he didn't.

'Don't listen to those people,' Callie cried, throwing her arms round Inspector Cheddar's neck. 'They don't know anything.'

'Really?' Inspector Cheddar sniffed.

'Definitely,' Michael agreed. 'You'll catch the villain, Dad. Don't worry. We know you will.'

Atticus was listening closely. He'd got it all mixed up! Now he understood. Michael only wanted there to be burglaries so that his dad would look good when he solved them!

'How?' Inspector Cheddar tried to smile. 'He doesn't leave any clues.'

'He'll make a mistake,' Michael said. 'Criminals always do, don't they, Atticus?'

Atticus purred weakly. Most criminals might make mistakes. But *he* never did. Inspector Cheddar didn't stand a chance against him and Jimmy Magpie's gang. He'd never solve the crimes. The Tofflys would call him mean names. People would laugh at him in the street. The Chief Inspector of Bigsworth would put him on traffic duty. Worst of all, Michael would be disappointed and Callie would be sad.

Mrs Tucker came in with a steaming cup of fish tea. 'Here, this will put hairs on your chest,' she beamed. 'I always give it to Mr Tucker before he sets sail in case he meets a *you-know-what*.'

Inspector Cheddar sniffed it suspiciously. His eyes watered.

'Any chance of a biscuit?' he asked.

'I might have some plankton-and-cod cookies.' Mrs Tucker went off to look for them.

Inspector Cheddar took a sip of tea. 'YUK!' he spluttered. He poured it out of the window.

Atticus thought he heard a faint squawk but the children were giggling and he couldn't be sure. Besides, his mind was on other things.

'Don't tell Mrs Tucker I did that,' Inspector Cheddar whispered.

Mrs Tucker came back with some green-looking biscuits. She eyed the empty cup. 'You'll be running around like one of those superheroes in a minute – Crabman, or whatever his name is,' she said, looking pleased.

Michael stifled a laugh.

Callie pretended to cough.

Inspector Cheddar sprang off the sofa. The fish tea seemed to have worked. Suddenly he *did* feel much better. 'Thank you, kids. Thank you, Mrs Tucker. Thank you, Atticus.'

'Where are you going?' the children wanted to know.

'I'm going back to the station.' Inspector Cheddar stuck his cap on jauntily. 'To catch a burglar.'

'Good luck, Dad!' Callie shouted after him.

'Yeah, go get him, Dad!' Michael yelled. He picked up Atticus lumpily and waved one of his paws towards Inspector Cheddar. 'Atticus says good luck too!'

The door slammed.

Feeling miserable, Atticus meowed to get down.

'What's wrong, Atticus?' Michael sounded concerned. 'You normally love being picked up.'

'Tummy-ache, probably.' Mrs Tucker said briskly. 'Now let's get your reading done.' She took the children into the kitchen.

Atticus slunk upstairs. He wriggled under the bed, wondering what on earth he was going to do.

1·2

'Chaka-chaka-chaka-chaka!'

Thug and Slasher were having fun. Jimmy was out and they were trying on some of the stolen jewellery. The sunlight, which came in bright stripes through the wooden planks of the old pier, made the precious stones sparkle like fireworks.

'What do you think?' Thug chattered, parading up and down the metal beams with a bracelet over one wing. 'Do emeralds suit me?'

'Without a doubt, Thug,' Slasher said. 'They go with your plumage.'

'I like you in rubies,' Thug returned the compliment. 'They suit your complexion.'

'Nah . . . you're just being polite.' Slasher grinned. 'You know what they say, Thug . . .' He threw the ruby necklace carelessly on to the brimming nest and picked out a ring with his beak. ' . . . Diamonds are a bird's best friend.'

'You crack me up, Slasher!' Thug nearly fell off the beam with laughing.

'CHAKA-CHAKA-CHAKA-CHAKA!'
There was a rush of wings.

Thug froze.

Slasher blinked nervously.

It was Jimmy Magpie.

'Jimmy!' Slasher tried to hide the diamond ring under his wing. 'We was just . . . er . . . checking things.'

'Put the stuff back.' Jimmy glared at the two magpies coldly. 'Do you want the fuzz to see you?'

'The fuzz?' Thug repeated.

'The cops. The heat. The bill.'

Thug and Slasher looked blank.

'The police, you idiots!' Jimmy squawked. 'They're out on patrol. Looking for the burglar.'

'The police!' gasped Thug.

'Yeah. I've been keeping an eye on them all day while you two have been playing at dressing up.' His eyes glittered brightly. 'Inspector Cheddar. He's in charge.'

'Cheddar?' gasped Slasher. 'Isn't that the name of

the lady who's organising the Toffly Hall antiques fair? The one who lives at number 2 Blossom Crescent.'

'Her husband,' Jimmy confirmed. 'I followed him back home this afternoon and listened at the window.' Jimmy glanced behind him and fanned his luminous-green tail feathers. 'I nearly got my tail scalded by some foul-smelling brew in the process.'

Thug looked nervous. 'You don't think he's on to us, do you?'

'Why would he be?' Jimmy demanded. 'What have you done?'

'Slasher tried to steal his badge.' Thug confessed.

'YOU DID WHAT?' Jimmy grabbed the diamond ring off Slasher and whacked him over the head with it. 'YOU BIRD BRAIN!'

'It wasn't me, it was him!' Slasher pushed Thug violently.

Thug fell off his perch, fluttered unsteadily, then landed on Slasher's back. 'No, it wasn't, it was you!'

Slasher pushed him off.

Thug shoved him back.

'Cut it out!' Jimmy snapped. 'Luckily, Inspector Cheddar's even more stupid than you two. He's no threat. Not yet, anyway. He hasn't got a clue about the burglaries. He's stumped.'

'Phew!' Thug put his wing round Slasher and hugged him. 'That's all right, then.'

'I did learn something interesting though,' Jimmy went on carefully, examining his tail in the glittering diamond, 'about our *so-called friend*, Atticus Claw.'

'What?' Slasher asked.

'He's living with the Cheddars.'

'No way!' Thug fell off his perch again.

'I don't believe it!' Slasher gasped.

'I got a peek through the window,' Jimmy said. 'He looked mighty cosy curled up next to the Inspector and a couple of snotty kids. Purring away, he was, like a good little kitty.'

Slasher stared at his boss. 'What's he up to?'

Jimmy's eyes gleamed. 'I'm not sure. My guess is it's to do with Toffly Hall antiques fair. Somehow he must have heard about it when he arrived. I reckon he's sneaked in there with the Cheddars so he can find out if there's going to be anything worth stealing.' He put his head on one side and looked sharply at the other magpies. 'You haven't told him about it, have you?' His voice was brimming with menace.

'No!' squawked Slasher.

'Definitely not!' Thug started to tremble. 'You can trust us!'

'I hope so,' Jimmy said icily. 'Or you know what will happen.' He tossed the ring back into the nest.

Slasher's beak twitched.

Thug's knees knocked.

'No, Jimmy, please . . .'

'Not the crows, Jimmy. Please! We haven't told the cat anything, I swear.' Tears were rolling down Thug's cheeks.

'Then he's cleverer than I thought,' Jimmy spat. 'Where better to get the lowdown on the antiques fair than in the organiser's own home? And where better to hide from the police than right under their noses?'

'What do you think he's going to do, Boss?' Thug asked timidly, rubbing his bruised ankle with his wing.

'He's after that tiara,' Jimmy said thoughtfully. 'Think about it; it could buy him all the mackerel in the Mediterranean.' He paused, his eyes glittering. 'What worries me is that the only way he can be sure of getting it is if we're out of the way . . .'

'You mean he's going to chomp us?' Thug gulped.

'Then he'd get everything!' Slasher fumed.

'Maybe,' Jimmy said. 'But he'd have to catch us first.'

'I'd biff him in the snout,' Thug said proudly.

'And I'd peck him in the eye.' Slasher sounded excited.

'He'd have you both for breakfast,' Jimmy said coldly. 'But I doubt he'd take me on in a hurry.'

'Who would, Boss?' Thug agreed. 'You're horrible.'

'Thanks, Thug.' Jimmy looked pleased. 'But even if he *does* manage to get rid of us, he's still got to snatch the tiara. Toffly Hall will be swarming with cops. Nah . . .' Jimmy shook his head. 'I think he's got something else in mind. Something much more devious.'

'What?' Slasher and Thug gawped at him.

'I think he's gonna frame us for the burglaries. Then, when Inspector Cheddar thinks the criminals are safely behind bars, he's going to walk into that antiques fair and steal Lady Toffly's tiara from under his nose.' He shrugged. 'That's what I'd do, anyway, if I were him.'

'I don't want to go to jail!' Fat tears rolled down Thug's cheeks. His body shook with sobs.

'Don't worry, Thug,' Jimmy said kindly. 'It won't come to that.' He took a deep breath and let out a satisfied sigh. 'Thanks to me, you won't be going to jail. Nor will Slasher . . .'

'Thanks, Boss!' Slasher sounded relieved.

'. . . and most importantly, nor will I.' Jimmy sat back comfortably against the nest and folded his wings. 'Atticus Claw, on the other hand, can look forward to a life sentence at Her Majesty's pleasure.'

Thug and Slasher looked at him, puzzled. 'But how, Boss?'

'We're going to give that cat a taste of his own medicine.' Jimmy smiled cruelly. 'We're going to turn the tables on him.' He leaned forward and spread his wings around the two magpies, gathering them close. His voice fell to a whisper. 'It's not *him* who's gonna frame *us*, boys. It's *us* who are gonna frame *him*!'

13

When the children had finished tea and gone upstairs for their baths, Atticus went out for a walk. He wanted to think about things.

After a while he found himself wandering along the beachfront past the shops. The weather had turned much warmer and quite a few families were sitting on the wall, eating ice creams. A boy was examining pebbles on the sand while a little girl paddled in the waves.

He made his way along the promenade towards the beach huts. To get there, he had to pass the pier. Luckily a small fairground had sprung up at one end of the car park since his last visit to the seaside. Atticus was glad. He didn't like the blaring music but at least it made it less likely the magpies would see him. The last thing he wanted right now was to bump into Jimmy and his gang. He skirted the fair-ground and sneaked past the end of the pier, threading his way round the back of some parked cars.

There was no sign of the magpies.

When he got to the beach huts he bumped into Mimi, the pretty Burmese.

'There you are!' she said. 'I was beginning to think you'd never come!'

Atticus hung his head. 'Sorry,' he said gruffly. Secretly, though, he was pleased to see her. 'You haven't really been waiting for me all this time, have you?'

'Of course not,' Mimi said shortly. 'I like coming down here to watch the children.' She began to clean her whiskers with a delicate front paw. 'Sometimes it gets a bit lonely at home. Aisha, my owner, doesn't have any kids. And she's out a lot of the time at work.'

'What does she do?' Atticus asked.

'She's a florist.' Mimi told him proudly. 'She owns a beautiful shop on the High Street. She has to get up really early to go to the market in Bigsworth to collect the flowers to make into bouquets; then in the evenings she delivers them in the van.' Mimi sighed. 'I'd never leave her, of course, but sometimes I think it would be fun to belong to a family.'

Atticus said nothing.

'Busy week?' Mimi asked, looking at him sideways.

'Fairly,' Atticus said non-commitally.

'Did you know we were burgled the other night?'

'I . . . er . . .' Atticus felt his whiskers burn.

'Someone stole Aisha's best necklace,' Mimi went on. 'She was very upset. Her mother gave it to her. It's made of emeralds.'

Atticus's good ear drooped.

'It happened while I was here . . .' Mimi paused . . . 'waiting for *you*.'

Atticus tried to look away but Mimi's golden eyes bored into his. 'You stole it, didn't you?'

Atticus sighed. Yes,' he said heavily. 'I did.'

Mimi stared out to sea. 'Do you want to tell me why?' she asked quietly.

All of a sudden Atticus found himself telling Mimi everything. He told her about Monte Carlo and Milan. He told her about Madrid and Montreal. He told her about Moscow and Miami. He told her about the message from the magpies and how he came to be in Littleton-on-Sea. Finally he told her about the Cheddars. 'I really like them,' he said help-lessly, 'and I've let them down. For a few measly sardines. And it's not just the Cheddars, is it? I didn't mean to upset your owner, or anyone else for that matter. I just never let myself think about it before. I've been a cat burglar all my life. I didn't want to get involved. Now, I'm not so sure.'

Mimi was quiet for a long time. 'Poor Atticus,' she said eventually, taking his paw. 'What are you going to do?'

Atticus glanced back towards the pier. He pictured the magpies crowing over their nest full of loot. The thought of Jimmy's cruel black eyes made him shiver.

'Well?' Mimi said.

Atticus let go of Mimi's paw and straightened his handkerchief. He'd made up his mind.

'I'm going to tell the magpies I want out,' he said. 'I'm going to tell them what we're doing is wrong. I'm going to tell them it has to stop. I'll go to the pier tomorrow morning when the kids are at school.'

Mimi smiled. 'And then?' she prompted.

'And then I'm going to return the jewellery to its owners – every single last piece of it, starting with Aisha.'

Mimi nuzzled his whiskers. 'I hoped you'd say that,' she purred.

They said goodbye. Mimi waved. Atticus tried to smile. It felt good to do the right thing for once. But it didn't really change anything, he thought sadly. He'd still have to leave. If the Cheddars ever found out what he'd done they'd never forgive him. And he couldn't forgive himself. He didn't deserve friends like Mimi. Or a loving family like the Cheddars. He sat alone for a long time watching the sunset until it was completely dark. Then he set out for Blossom Crescent with a heavy heart. Once he'd seen to it that everything had returned to normal in Littleton-on-Sea, he would leave number 2 Blossom Crescent and return to Monte Carlo where he couldn't cause any more trouble.

🐾

Michael and Callie had just had their baths when the doorbell rang.

'Do your teeth,' Mrs Tucker ordered, 'while I see who it is.'

The children waited for her to go downstairs, then they crept out of the bathroom and sat on the stairs in their dressing gowns peering through the banisters.

A lady in a pink sundress and floppy hat was standing on the doorstep next to a small bald man with a moustache. He was wearing sunglasses and carrying a suitcase.

'We want to talk to Inspector Cheddar,' the man said abruptly. 'It's about the burglaries.'

'He's out,' Mrs Tucker said. 'You could try the police station.'

The woman shook her head. 'He's not there either,' she said.

'He's probably following up an important lead,' Mrs Tucker said, 'on the trail of the burglar.'

'He'd better be,' the man snapped. 'My name is Pearson – we were the first victims of that greedy fiend!'

Callie clutched Michael's hand.

'Shall I ask the Inspector to call you in the morning?' Mrs Tucker asked.

'No point,' Mr Pearson said tersely. 'We're going on a cruise. It's not safe here.' He looked about anxiously, as though he expected the burglar to jump out from behind a bush and steal his moustache. 'Come on, Elspeth, I told you it was a waste of time.' He took hold of his wife's arm.

Mrs Pearson shook him off. 'No, Stanley. It might be important.'

Mr Pearson gave a grunt.

'What might?' Mrs Tucker asked quickly.

'I remembered something about the burglary,' Mrs Pearson said. 'I think it could be a clue.'

Michael and Callie looked at one another excitedly. They edged forward.

'Did you see something?' Mrs Tucker asked.

'Well, there was a cat,' Mrs Pearson said, frowning. 'Just beneath the window.'

'Ugly-looking brute,' Mr Pearson added. 'It looked as if it had been fighting. One of its ears was all chewed.'

Michael and Callie looked at one another. '*Atticus?*' Callie whispered anxiously.

The same thought had obviously occurred to Mrs Tucker. 'Was it wearing a red handkerchief round its neck?' she asked sharply.

'Definitely not,' Mr Pearson answered curtly.

'*Phew!*' Michael sighed with relief.

'But it wasn't what I *saw* that might be important, Stanley; it was what I *heard*.' Mrs Pearson interrupted firmly. 'The window was open a little and there was a strange noise outside. It woke me up.' She leaned forwards. 'I think it might have been the burglar,' she hissed.

'What did it sound like?' Mrs Tucker demanded.

'Well, it's hard to describe . . .'

Mr Pearson looked at his watch impatiently. 'Come on, Elspeth, spit it out! We haven't got all night,' he grumbled.

'It was a sort of chattering,' Mrs Pearson glared at him. '. . . Really loud.' She paused. 'I know this sounds daft but . . .' She lowered her voice . . . 'it was as though someone was *laughing* at us.'

'Daft is right,' Mr Pearson said tetchily. 'I mean, what burglar would start chattering and laughing just after breaking and entering a house and stealing all the jewels?!'

'I don't know.' Mrs Pearson sounded deflated. 'I just thought I should tell the Inspector anyway, just in case.'

'Quite right.' Mrs Tucker glared at Mr Pearson. 'Otherwise he'd arrest you for withholding information and throw you both in jail. Have a nice trip.' She closed the front door.

'Chattering.' She scratched her head. 'That's odd.' She started up the stairs.

Michael and Callie jumped up. They hurried back into the bathroom and grabbed their toothbrushes.

Mrs Tucker reached the bathroom door and sur-

veyed them critically. 'What do you two make of all that?'

The children tried to look innocent.

'Make of what?' Michael spat toothpaste into the basin.

'Don't try that on me, Michael Cheddar,' Mrs Tucker said firmly. 'I know you were eavesdropping. Your teeth would have fallen out by now if you'd been brushing them that long.' She bustled them into the bedroom and started to plait Callie's hair. 'Well?' She repeated.

'I don't understand.' Callie was the first to speak. 'I mean why would the burglar start chatting?'

'It wasn't *chatting* Mrs Pearson heard,' Mrs Tucker said carefully, securing Callie's plait with an elastic. 'It was chatt-*er*-ing.'

'You mean like the magpies when they tried to steal Dad's badge?' Michael said without thinking.

Mrs Tucker stared at him. 'Holy coley, Michael Cheddar!' she whispered. 'You're a genius.'

'Wait a minute . . .' Michael stared at her, astonished. 'You don't really think the burglar could be a *bird*, do you?'

'Not just *any* bird,' Mrs Tucker told him sternly. 'A *magpie*. They're different. I told you the other day. They love stealing things. You saw what they're capable of. I wouldn't put anything past them. Flying round burgling houses sounds exactly like the sort of thing they'd get up to after dark.'

'Are they really clever enough to open safes?' Callie's eyes were round.

'Definitely,' Mrs Tucker replied. 'Those magpies are criminal masterminds, you can bet your barnacles.'

'But how do they get in?' Michael demanded. 'Dad said the windows in some of the houses were closed.'

'They must have found another way.' Mrs Tucker rubbed her chin. 'Something a magpie could get through but a human couldn't.'

'What about a cat flap?' Callie suggested. 'Like Atticus uses?'

'Brilliant, Callie Cheddar!' Mrs Tucker shouted. 'You're a chip off the old block. Magpies. Cat flaps. It all fits. What a team of super sleuths we are!' She gave them both a bear hug. 'I can't wait to tell your dad. He'll be as happy as a hake when he finds out we've solved the case.' She glanced at her watch. It was nine o'clock. 'Now, into bed! You've got your school trip tomorrow. I'd better get down to the kitchen and make you a packed lunch. Goodnight!'

The children got into bed.

'Where's Atticus?' Callie asked sleepily.

'He went out.' Michael yawned. 'I don't think he's back yet.'

'Maybe he's gone to catch the magpies . . .' Callie hardly managed to finish the sentence before she fell asleep.

Michael lay awake. He wondered if the two magpies that had tried to steal Dad's badge really could be responsible for the spate of burglaries – the scrawny one with the hooked foot and the fat one with feathers missing from its tail. If it came to an identity parade he was pretty sure he'd recognise them again. He imagined them hopping into houses through the cat flap and picking safes with their beaks, then flying away into the night with the jewellery in their claws.

If Mrs Tucker was right, somewhere in Littleton-on-Sea was a magpie nest stuffed with necklaces and bracelets, watches and rings. All Dad had to do was find it and arrest the birds. He'd be a hero. Everyone would be proud of him, especially the Chief Inspector of Bigsworth. The Tofflys would shut up. The antiques fair would go ahead. Mum would have a chance of getting the job she wanted. Dad might even get a call from Scotland Yard.

Michael kicked the duvet restlessly. There was just one BIG problem. Dad didn't really *get* animals. He didn't like them much and he certainly didn't think there was anything clever about them. What if Dad didn't *believe* Mrs Tucker? What if he thought she was being superstitious about the magpies? *What if he thought she was being ridiculous?* Somehow Michael didn't think he'd be as happy as a hake the next morning when Mrs Tucker told him her idea. In fact, he didn't think he'd be very happy at all.

A few minutes later Michael heard a gentle *thwump* at the foot of his bed. He felt the mattress sag a little beside his feet and something soft squish his toes where they stuck out of the bottom of the duvet.

'Hi, Atticus, I'm glad you're here.' Michael reached down and stroked him. 'But if I were you, I'd keep out of the way at breakfast time,' he whispered sleepily. 'I've got a feeling Dad isn't going to be in a very good mood.'

CHOMP! CHOMP! CHOMP!

The next morning, when Atticus came downstairs, Inspector Cheddar was crunching toast noisily. Atticus peered at him from the safety of the doorway. Michael was right. The Inspector *was* in a bad mood – terrible actually, if the thunderous expression on his face was anything to go by.

Atticus glanced around the kitchen.

Mrs Cheddar had already left for work.

The kids were sitting at the table looking miserable.

Mrs Tucker was standing beside the sink with a frying pan in her hand looking as if she was about to bash someone with it.

Atticus quaked at the sight of her. Mrs Tucker's mouth was drawn in a tight line. Her forehead was wrinkled into waves. Her frizzy grey hair was standing on end and she was grinding her teeth unpleasantly.

She glowered at Inspector Cheddar.

Inspector Cheddar glowered back.

It was obvious the two of them had had a row.

Atticus wondered what it could have been about. They had seemed chummy enough yesterday over plankton-and-cod cookies. Perhaps Mrs Tucker had found out Inspector Cheddar had thrown away her fish tea.

Atticus slunk over to his bowl and stared at it hopefully. No one had thought to put anything in it. Not even the children. He waited. Nobody moved. Nobody spoke. The heavy silence was broken only by the sound of crashing crockery as Mrs Tucker banged down the frying pan and started to clear the table – slinging empty bowls and cups recklessly into the sink.

Atticus kept staring at the empty dish. Eventually he heard Mrs Tucker open a cupboard with a crash. She rattled round in a drawer. There followed an unpleasant scraping noise that set his teeth on edge. What was she doing? He didn't dare look. Atticus's stomach gurgled. *Couldn't anyone see he was about to starve to death?*

Mrs Tucker bent down beside him.

Food! He thought. *At last!*

SPLAT!

A thick cylinder of evil-smelling wobbly pink goo landed heavily in Atticus's dish and collapsed into a pile of lumpy sludge.

Atticus flinched as a dollop splattered on to his clean whiskers. He wiped it off with a paw. *Tinned food? TINNED FOOD?* Atticus couldn't believe it. *What had happened to his sardines?* Or those yummy foil sachets Callie bought him? He *hated* tinned food. It was worse than the mummified rabbit poo the matador from Madrid used to feed him.

Atticus was about to walk away when Mrs Tucker's hostile glare fell upon him. He stopped.

'That's all we've got, you fussy animal!' she snapped. 'Eat it up!'

Atticus tiptoed back to his bowl. *Why was everyone in such a bad mood?!* He didn't dare leave it though. He chewed his way reluctantly through gristle and fat, trying hard not to burp. He hoped he wouldn't get indigestion.

'Bye, Atticus,' Michael said dolefully, getting down from the table.

'See you later.' Callie gave his ears a stroke.

Atticus couldn't purr. A piece of gristle was stuck in his throat.

The children went to put on their shoes in the hall. From the corner of his eye, Atticus saw Mrs Tucker give Inspector Cheddar one last furious scowl and march after them, clutching two brightly coloured plastic containers, one in each hand. *Why had they got those? Where were they going?* Atticus was worried that the kids had left their school bags beside the kitchen table but no one else seemed to care. He tried to meow but his gums were glued together with gunk.

The front door slammed. Mrs Tucker and the children had gone.

Atticus spat out what was left in his mouth. He picked a bit of fat from his teeth with one claw and had a drink of water.

Meanwhile Inspector Cheddar was finishing his cereal. He drained his mug of tea, banged it down on the table, picked up his cap and jammed it on his head. He got up and strode towards the kitchen door.

Atticus stared after him. Inspector Cheddar had a wet patch on the back of his trousers where he'd sat in something.

'Meow,' Atticus yowled urgently. It seemed only

fair to tell him. The Chief Inspector of Bigsworth wouldn't be very impressed if Inspector Cheddar turned up to work with a soggy bum.

'Shut up, you mangy moggy!' Inspector Cheddar yelled. 'I've had just about enough animal nonsense for one morning!' He stormed out.

What animal nonsense? Atticus stopped in mid-meow. He felt confused. Yesterday it was tickles and sardines. Today it was shouting and tinned cat food. He sighed. He'd never understand humans. Perhaps it was just as well he was going away.

The front door slammed again. He was alone.

Atticus tried to concentrate on the day ahead. He looked at the kitchen clock. It was 8.15. The magpies had called him to the pier at 11.15 to discuss the next stage of the crime spree; exactly eight days to the hour since their first meeting. Jimmy and his gang seemed to be enjoying the burglaries. They'd even talked about building a new nest to hold some more jewels. They wouldn't enjoy what he had to say to them today though – that was for sure.

15

The school trip was an outing to the fair beside the pier.

Callie and Michael found a quiet spot by the candyfloss stall and sat down on a bench.

'This morning was awful!' Callie began. 'I've never seen Dad so cross.'

'I know!' Michael said. 'And Mrs Tucker looked as though she'd swallowed a bottle of vinegar.' He sighed. 'I had a feeling Dad wouldn't believe her.'

'You were right,' Callie said. 'When Dad asked her if she needed to lie down I thought she was going to hit him with the frying pan!'

'She got her own back though,' Michael said, 'when she spread that fish paste on his chair.'

'What are we going to do?' Callie said. 'Dad will never catch the magpies if he doesn't believe they did it.'

Michael stared gloomily out to sea. 'Hey look!' He narrowed his eyes. 'Isn't that Atticus?'

Callie jumped up. A large tabby cat with four white socks and a chewed ear was picking its way across the sand from the direction of the beach huts towards the pier. It had a red handkerchief around its neck.

'What's he doing here?' Michael wondered. 'Do you think he's lost?'

'Maybe he's looking for the magpies!' Callie said excitedly.

'Don't be silly,' Michael said. 'How would Atticus know about the magpies?'

'Beats me,' Callie said, 'but I'm going to follow him, just in case. And anyway, I don't want him to get lost again.' She started to move away. 'Come on.'

'We can't!' Michael was horrified. 'What if the teachers find out we're missing?'

'I don't care,' Callie said stubbornly. She jumped down on to the sand.

'Callie,' Michael shouted. 'Come back!'

Callie kept on going.

Michael groaned. Little sisters could be a real pain sometimes. He glanced round. No one was looking. 'OK,' he muttered. 'I'm coming.' He ran after Callie. 'Wait for me!'

'Hurry up!' Callie called back. 'Or we'll lose him.'

Michael jumped down from the sea wall on to the sand. He raced to catch her. 'Where's he gone now?' he panted.

A dog started to bark.

'Over there.' Callie pointed to Atticus's waving tail. Luckily the dog was on a lead. It couldn't chase Atticus even though it wanted to. 'He's heading for the pier.'

They ran after Atticus. The sand was soft and their trainers kept sinking into it, making them stumble. Atticus was making quicker progress than they were – picking his way effortlessly along the sand. He paused for a second and sniffed the air. Then he disappeared into the dark shadows beneath the pier.

'Quick!' Callie urged Michael. 'We're losing him.'

They stumbled on until they got to the pier. They had walked along it loads of times with their parents but they had never been *underneath* it before.

'It's creepy!' Callie whispered nervously, peering into the dark space.

The sea crashed in and out of the shadows. The air was rank with the smell of mouldy seaweed.

'It stinks!' Michael pulled a face. He couldn't help thinking that any minute now one of Mr Tucker's giant sea monsters would slither out from behind a rock!

'Chaka-chaka-chaka-chaka!'

The sound of chattering came from somewhere up ahead.

MAGPIES!

'That's them!' Callie gripped Michael's hand. 'I knew Atticus was on their trail.'

Michael frowned. It was the magpies all right. Nothing else could make that horrible noise. But why would Atticus be following them? 'I still don't see how . . .' he began.

'Shhh!' Callie tugged her brother's arm. 'Come on.'

They tiptoed forwards.

'CHAKA-CHAKA-CHAKA-CHAKA!'

The chattering came again, louder this time.

'How many of them do you think there are?' Callie whispered.

'I don't know,' Michael hissed back. 'Two, maybe? Three? He looked around. *Where was Atticus?*

Suddenly they heard a low throaty moan, followed by a sharp meow and some fierce hissing.

'Look! Up there!' Callie pointed.

Michael peered up into the gloom. Way above him, where the light shone through the gaps in the pier's wooden platform, he could just make out a scruffy mess of twigs and leaves sandwiched between the iron beams. Michael gasped. Shiny strings of red, gold and dazzling white dangled from it like wonky Christmas lights, glinting in the narrow shafts of sun. A silver watchstrap hung lopsidedly over the edge.

'It's the stolen jewellery!' Callie breathed. 'Atticus found it! I told you he would!'

'CHAKA-CHAKA-CHAKA-CHAKA-CHAKA.' The magpies were going mental. One of them – a huge bird with a glossy green tail and blue wings – took off for a moment and circled the air, its eyes shining cruelly in the light reflected by the jewels.

'That must be the leader,' Michael whispered, pulling Callie back. The bird looked vicious. Its beak was as sharp as a dagger. Luckily it was so intent on

120

whatever was happening beside the nest it didn't notice them.

'GGRRRRRRR.' It wasn't a purr. It was a growl.

'That's Atticus,' Callie hissed.

Michael's eyes travelled slowly along the beam. Beside the nest dangled a long furry striped tail he recognised. It twitched backwards and forwards slowly.

'GGRRRRRR.' The growl came again.

'He's arguing with the magpies!' Callie whispered.

Suddenly Atticus's tail disappeared.

'Quick, Callie, he's coming down.' Michael pulled her out of sight.

Atticus dropped down on to the sand a few feet away from their hiding place. Michael and Callie stared. Instead of the red handkerchief being tied round his neck, Atticus was carrying it in his mouth by its four corners. From one side of the untidy package dangled the end of a green sparkling necklace.

Michael felt the colour drain from his face. He watched Atticus pad away into the sunshine. Then he stumbled out from underneath the pier.

Callie ran after him. 'What's the matter?'

'Atticus is working with the magpies,' Michael

gasped. 'He's involved in the burglaries.'

'No!' Callie protested. 'I don't believe you!'

'Remember what the Pearsons said? It all makes sense.'

Callie shook her head stubbornly.

'Mrs Pearson saw a cat beside the bedroom window,' Michael said urgently.

'So?'

'Mr Pearson said it looked as if it had been fighting. He said it had a chewed ear.'

Callie went white. 'So does Atticus,' she whispered.

'Exactly. We thought it couldn't be him because he wasn't wearing his handkerchief,' Michael went on. 'But what if he'd taken it off to hold the jewels?'

Callie screwed her fists into her ears. 'I don't want to listen,' she said.

'*That's* how he knew where to find the magpies, Callie,' Michael said. 'Because he's a *cat burglar*. He's been helping them. *He's* the one who's been using the cat flaps to break into people's houses.'

Callie's eyes filled with tears. 'You're not going to tell Dad, are you?'

'I have to!' Michael said despairingly. 'Atticus is in a lot of trouble. He's a thief! What he's done is wrong.'

'But Dad will put him in jail,' Callie wailed. 'Can't we just tell Dad we found the jewels? Can't we just tell him it was the magpies?'

'No, Callie. We can't. It wouldn't be true. And anyway, what if Atticus does it again?'

'I know, but . . .' Callie buried her head in her arms and started to sob.

'CHAKA-CHAKA-CHAKA-CHAKA!'

'CHAKA-CHAKA-CHAKA-CHAKA!'

The magpies were still chattering furiously.

Callie looked up. 'Then why are the magpies so cross?' she sniffed. 'If Atticus is supposed to be helping them?'

'I'm not sure,' Michael said slowly. A crazy idea had occurred to him. *What if* . . .

'Maybe Atticus has changed his mind,' Callie said suddenly. 'Maybe he doesn't want to be a cat burglar any more.'

'That's just what I was thinking!' Michael jumped up from the sand. 'Come on, let's follow him and see where he goes next!' He ran off.

Callie scrambled up and chased after him.

Atticus was padding along the beach towards

the promenade. He jumped on to the sea wall, crossed over by the bus stop and started walking up the road towards the centre of town.

The children hung back until they were sure Atticus wouldn't see them, then they leapt over the wall, crossed the road carefully and tiptoed after him. After a little while Atticus turned right into a quiet street just off the main road. He walked along it a short way and disappeared behind a hedge.

'He's gone into that garden!' Callie hissed.

'Quick!' Michael ran to the gate. 'We need to see exactly what he's doing.' He peered over the gate just in time to see Atticus's tail disappearing round the back of the cottage. Michael opened the gate quietly and sneaked in. Callie followed him. They peered round the side of the house into the back garden.

'Oh, look,' Callie gasped. 'There's another cat!'

A small caramel-coloured cat with a chocolate-brown face was sunbathing on the patio. She got up when she saw Atticus. Atticus dropped his bundle and pushed the corners of the handkerchief away with one paw.

'He's showing her the necklace!' Michael said.

The caramel-coloured cat meowed.

124

'You don't think he's *giving* it to her, do you?' Callie said doubtfully.

'No. I don't think so.' Michael shook his head. 'Look, he's wrapping it up.'

Atticus dropped the necklace back into the handkerchief and picked it up again. The children watched breathlessly as he followed the small cat towards the house. They disappeared through the cat flap.

Michael's heart was beating fast. 'What's he doing now?' He grabbed Callie's hand. Together, they crept along the back of the house and peeked into the kitchen.

Atticus had jumped on to the kitchen table. Beside him was a handbag. He placed the handkerchief carefully on the table and drew the corners to one side with his teeth. Gently, he lifted the necklace up with one paw. The emeralds glinted in the sun. Atticus flicked out his claws one by one. He twiddled the clasp of the handbag. It sprung open. Carefully, Atticus placed the necklace in the handbag and snapped it shut. He picked up the handkerchief in his mouth and jumped off the table.

Michael and Callie ran to the front of the cottage and back out to the pavement. They were both laughing.

'He put it back!' Michael yelled, hugging his sister. 'He put it back!'

'He's not bad after all!' Callie cried in delight.

Just then they heard the sound of voices.

'There they are!' Two very cross-looking teachers were on the corner of the main road. They started towards them.

Michael and Callie looked on in horror. They had completely forgotten they were supposed to be on the school outing!

'Uh-oh,' Michael groaned. 'Now we're for it!'

16

Beneath the pier, Jimmy Magpie was hopping up and down the rusty beam in a rage.

'I knew that cat couldn't be trusted!' he screeched.

'You was right, Boss!' Slasher said hastily, moving a safe distance away.

'Yeah, Boss, you hit the tail on the head!' Thug agreed.

'NAIL! You idiot. Not tail. I hit the *nail* on the head.' Jimmy swiped at him with his beak.

Thug dodged and fell off the beam in a flutter of feathers. 'Chaka-chaka-chaka-chaka.'

'But even I didn't think he'd be capable of such snivelling cowardice!'

'It's pathetic!' Slasher said.

'Sick!' agreed Thug. 'You should have seen your

face, Boss, when the cat said he wanted to put all the loot back!'

'You looked like you'd been told you'd got bird flu!' Slasher chortled.

'And then when he took that necklace,' Thug hooted. 'I thought you were going to lay an egg!'

THWAK! Jimmy punched them both in the crop.

'He took me by surprise, you idiots, or I'd have stopped him.' Jimmy paced up and down. 'What a wussy pussy!' he screeched. 'What a pampered pet!' He put on a baby voice. 'Poor little kitty-witty, doesn't like being a cat burglar any more. Wants us to say sorry and give the jewels back to their owners like good little magpies.' He picked up an old sardine from a heap beside the nest and bashed it viciously on the twigs until its head fell off. 'NEVER!!' he screeched. 'NEVER. NEVER. NEVER. NEVER. I'd rather be boiled in oil.'

'Er . . . I wouldn't,' Thug said nervously, regaining his perch. 'If it's all the same to you.'

'Nor me,' Slasher gurgled. 'I've never been good with boiling.'

'SHUT UP!' Jimmy hurled the rest of the sardine at Thug. Thug ducked. The sardine hit Slasher hard on the chest. He fell off the beam in a flap. 'You two

128

are the most lily-livered layabouts I have ever come across. You're a disgrace to the bird world. You're a pair of pathetic poultry. PUK-PUK-PUK-PUK-PUK-PUK-PUK!' Jimmy strutted along the beam with his wings tucked in like a chicken. 'You're like PIGEONS!' He turned on them. 'Remember Penguin? Remember Beaky? Remember Goon?'

'Yes, Boss.' Slasher crawled back on to the ledge and collapsed.

'They'd have been happy to be boiled in oil. They'd have laughed at the prospect. You could have pulled out all their feathers one by one and tied their beaks in a knot and they wouldn't have cared.'

'You sure, Boss?' Thug scratched his head. 'Only it doesn't sound much fun.'

'YES, I'M SURE, YOU FEATHER-BRAINED FATTY!' Jimmy's wing popped out in a swift karate chop and punched Thug in the stomach. 'It's not meant to be FUN. This is WAR. We're doing this to HURT HUMANS. Just like they hurt us.' He drew a claw across his throat. 'That cat's curtains.'

Thug gulped. 'You gonna get the crows in, Jimmy?' he whispered. 'Only, can I leave before they kill him? I don't like the sight of blood.'

129

'We don't need the crows,' Jimmy snapped, gouging an eyeball from the sardine head and squishing it. 'Atticus Grammaticus Cattypuss Claw may think he's so smart snuggling in with Inspector Cheddar and his cheesy little kids.' He snorted. 'Well, they're not going to help him. I'll teach him to climb up here and steal *my* jewellery.'

'We still gonna frame him, Boss?' Slasher grinned. He liked it when the boss got nasty as long as it wasn't with him. 'Even though he's not gonna take the tiara any more?'

'We sure are.' Jimmy squished the other eyeball. 'Like a bloomin' Picasso.'

'We're gonna frame him! We're gonna frame him!' Thug sang, jumping up and down, flapping his wings excitedly. 'YIPPEE!'

'He's going to jay-el! He's going to jay-el!' Slasher chanted, doing a little dance. 'HOORAY!'

Jimmy cackled. 'I can't wait to see the look on that cat's face when he gets arrested! Then, when Inspector Cheddar thinks he's got the thief safely behind bars, *we'll* swoop on the antiques fair and steal the Tofflys' tiara. And there's nothing Atticus Grammaticus Cattypuss GOODY-GOODY Claw can do about it.'

'Oh, Boss, you're so clever!' Thug said admiringly. 'Can I have your claw-tograph?'

'SHUT UP!' Jimmy yelled. 'Now get the plastic bag and fill it up with swag.'

Twenty minutes later Jimmy Magpie landed elegantly in the back garden of number 2 Blossom Crescent. Thug and Slasher tumbled head first after him and crash-landed in the rockery. The plastic bag was heavy. Their beaks ached from carrying it.

'You wait here. I'll check that the coast's clear.' Jimmy took off again and circled the house, checking in all the windows to see if anyone was there. He left the kitchen until last. His beady eyes glittered as he peered in from the window ledge.

'Over here!' Jimmy hissed. 'The cat basket's in the kitchen.' He fluttered down from the window and hopped towards the back door.

Thug and Slasher heaved the bag along the patio.

'Pick it up!' Jimmy ordered. 'We don't want it to burst!'

'There's not much "we" about it,' Thug grumbled. 'You're not doing anything!'

'Don't let him hear you say that!' Slasher hissed

131

'Or he'll pull our feathers out and boil us!'

Thug picked up the bag smartly.

The two magpies struggled towards the cat flap.

'I'll hold it.' Jimmy pushed it open with one powerful wing.

'Heave!' The birds swung the bag through the cat flap. It landed on the other side of the door with a loud CLINK.

Jimmy bowed at Thug and Slasher. 'Ladies first,' he said sarcastically.

'Thanks, Boss,' Thug said.

The magpies hopped in.

'Nice gaff!' Slasher said, gazing round the kitchen. 'Wouldn't mind living here myself.' He flew over to the washing machine. 'This would make a perfect nest if you put a few twigs in it.' He jumped in. 'Very cosy!'

'Here, let me help!' Thug closed the door. It gave a click. Slasher's face peered out of the drum. He tapped frantically at the glass with his beak. There was a muffled squawk. 'Help!' he yelled. 'I'm trapped! Let me out!'

Thug ignored him. 'Chaka-chaka-chaka-chaka!' He jumped into the laundry basket and bounced up and down on a pile of clean washing. 'A knicker trampoline!' he cried in delight. 'I'm in magpie heaven!' He picked out one of Inspector Cheddar's socks and pulled it over his head. 'Help!' he yelled, keeling over in fright. 'Somebody turned the lights out!'

'PACK IT IN!' Jimmy pulled the sock off Thug's head and pecked him.

'Let me out!' Slasher's voice came from inside the washing machine.

'YOU DODOS!' Jimmy flew on to the counter above the washing machine and bent his head forward over the control buttons. It wasn't at all obvious from upside down which one opened the door. Jimmy hesitated.

Thug landed beside Jimmy. 'It's this one, Boss,' he said confidently. 'Trust me, I'm a pro.' He leaned over and tapped a button with his beak.

There was a sound of running water. 'GLUGLUGLUGLUGLUGLUGLUG,' Slasher gurgled. 'WHOOAAOOAA . . .' The drum started to rotate.

'PUT THE JEWELS IN THE CAT BASKET,' Jimmy roared. 'Before I put YOU in the waste disposal!'

'All right,' Thug muttered. 'Keep your feathers on.' He fluttered to the floor and pushed Atticus's basket towards the plastic bag.

'Stuff them under the mattress,' Jimmy ordered, 'so it looks like he's been trying to hide them.'

Thug lifted the mattress with one foot and emptied the contents of the bag on to the base of the basket. Carefully he re-made Atticus's bed so that only a few inches of a diamond necklace were visible.

'Very nice, Thug,' Jimmy said approvingly. 'Very nice.'

Thug sighed. 'Thanks, Jimmy.' He eyed the necklace. The diamonds twinkled back at him. 'It's so lovely,' he sniffed. 'It seems such a waste to leave it here!'

'I know,' Jimmy said consolingly. 'But you've got to think of the bigger picture, Thug. Think of Atticus Claw in the slammer. Think of Beaky all mangled and mushed. Think of the Tofflys' tiara.'

'All the same . . .' Thug looked longingly at the diamonds.

'CHAKA-CHAKA-CHAKA-CHAKA-CHAKA!' Jimmy glanced at the washing machine. Slasher was still going round. 'Here, Thug,' he demanded. 'What time do kids finish school?'

''Bout three, Boss, I reckon,' Thug sniffed.

Jimmy looked at the kitchen clock. It was only one-thirty. 'We'd better stay here and keep a lookout in case the cat rocks up before the fun starts,' he said. 'We don't want him busting our plan.' He stretched out the tip of his wing towards the necklace. 'You know it does seem a pity,' he said, stroking the stones thoughtfully, 'to let the diamonds go for the sake of that cowardly cat. I wonder if there's anything we could put there instead.' Jimmy's eyes glittered. 'You don't suppose Mrs Cheddar has anything shiny up-stairs, do you?' he said slowly.

Thug's eyes gleamed. 'Bound to!' he said more cheerfully. 'Stands to reason, Boss, given how she's into antiques and all that.'

'That's what I was thinking,' Jimmy nodded. He put his wing round Thug. 'How about we go and take a look?'

Leaving a soggy Slasher to complete his cycle, they flew upstairs.

17

'So, it's a fight you want, do you?' Inspector Cheddar
was daydreaming. In the dream he was an expert at
karate. He'd just caught the burglar, who was dressed
in a Santa Claus suit with a sack marked BOOTY,
sneaking down a chimney. HI-YA! KER-CHUNG!
SMACK-POW! With a few clever kicks and chops
the burglar was at his mercy. Inspector Cheddar
whipped out the handcuffs. 'You're under arrest,
mate,' he whispered. Then he stared in disbelief. The
burglar had grown wings. In a flash he'd turned into
a black-and-white bird and flown back up the chimney and away, cackling loudly to himself.
'Chaka-chaka-chaka-chaka . . .'

'What are you babbling about now, Cheddar?'
The Chief Inspector of Bigsworth roared.

Inspector Cheddar woke with a start. He was in

the police station at Bigsworth puzzling over paper-work, not catching burglars at all! 'Sorry, sir!'

'You should be!' The Chief Inspector shouted. 'Your wife's on the phone. You need to get over to the school. The headmaster wants to see you. NOW!'

🐾

Mrs Cheddar was waiting for him in the headmaster's office. So were Callie and Michael.

'Dad!' Michael cried as soon as he saw him. 'We know where the stolen jewellery is!'

'It's under the pier, Dad!' Callie said excitedly. 'In the magpies' nest. We saw it!'

'Huh-hum.' The headmaster interrupted sternly.

Inspector Cheddar sat down opposite the head-master. He looked at Callie and Michael, puzzled. Callie's face was flushed. Michael had seaweed in his hair. Little piles of sand leaked out of their trainers on to the headmaster's floor. Inspector Cheddar couldn't understand it. They were clearly in trouble but they both looked as if it were Christmas.

'I'm afraid your children ruined the entire school outing,' the headmaster sighed. He was a kind man and he didn't like telling people off, but spoiling the school trip was going too far, even for him. 'It seems they decided to go off by themselves to do a bit of detective work when they were supposed to be on the dodgems.'

'But, Dad!' Michael protested. 'Mrs Tucker was right. The magpies *are* involved in the burglaries!'

'Huh-hum!' The headmaster interrupted again. 'Luckily, the alarm was raised before they got too far. Mrs Cooper, the Year 3 assistant, spotted them in Sea Shell Drive.'

'We saw Atticus!' Michael told him proudly. 'We followed him to the pier.'

'He was having a row with the magpies,' Callie gabbled. 'He'd taken off his handkerchief.'

'Without the handkerchief he answers the description the Pearsons gave of the cat they saw at the window!' Michael explained. 'He's been working with the magpies. He's been taking the jewels.'

'But don't worry, Dad,' Callie said quickly. 'He's not going to do it any more.'

'Obviously this is quite a serious matter,' the headmaster began again.

'He's changed his mind about being a burglar!' Callie rattled on. 'He's started to give things back!'

'We followed him to Sea Shell Drive,' Michael said. 'He returned the lady's emerald necklace!'

Callie swung her legs to and fro. 'We saw him, Dad!'

'Normally I'd involve the police when a child goes missing . . .' the headmaster said to Inspector Cheddar.

'Can't you see?!' Michael shouted. 'He's trying to say he's sorry!'

'But as you *are* the police,' the headmaster gave up. He had never known such rude children. 'I think on this occasion I'll just let you handle it.'

As soon as they got into the car, Michael and Callie started talking at once.

Inspector Cheddar held up his hand for silence. 'I don't want to hear another word about it!' he said in a dreadful voice. He turned the key in the ignition.

'But, Dad . . .'

'I said, ZIP IT!' he shouted. This was an expression Inspector Cheddar usually reserved for people who complained about parking tickets. Now he was using it on his own kids!

Callie started to cry.

Michael bit his lip. 'We were just trying to help,' he said quietly.

Mrs Cheddar glared at her husband. She put an arm round Callie.

Michael held her other hand.

'They might be telling the truth, you know!' she hissed. 'Have you thought about that? Maybe they're right. Maybe Atticus was the burglar, but now he's changed his mind. Maybe he *was* trying to say sorry. Maybe the magpies *are* involved. They tried to steal your badge, didn't they?'

Inspector Cheddar gripped the wheel. *Magpies! Nests full of stolen jewellery!* He'd never heard anything so ridiculous in his life. Everyone had gone mad since Atticus Grammaticus Cattypuss Claw arrived. He needed a cup of tea!

🐾

A few minutes later they pulled up outside number 2 Blossom Crescent. Mrs Cheddar let them out in silence and drove off back to Toffly Hall for the final preparations for the fair. Inspector Cheddar marched up the path and let himself in. He threw open the kitchen door and went to fill the kettle.

'WHOAOAOAO!' He tripped over the cat basket and banged his head on a cupboard. Inspector Cheddar swore. Atticus *again*! What was the cat basket doing there anyway? It was normally tucked away beside the fridge. He nudged it with his foot.

CLINK! Something clattered on to the tiled floor from beneath the spongy mattress. Inspector Cheddar stared. His wife's best brooch! What was that doing in the kitchen? She normally kept it upstairs in a jewellery case in their bedroom.

Inspector Cheddar bent down to pick it up. He examined the mattress. It was all lumpy and bumpy. Something else was hidden underneath. He picked it up gingerly. A tangled heap of jewellery tumbled out. His mouth fell open.

'Atticus!' he whispered. His face went green. 'So the children were right. It *was* you all along!'

Michael and Callie stood in the doorway aghast.

'No!' Callie cried. 'It's not Atticus's fault! We told you! He was stealing for the magpies! But he doesn't want to any more. He's taking things back!'

'He's changed his mind, Dad,' Michael yelled. 'I promise you, he didn't steal Mum's brooch!'

Just then Atticus's head appeared through the cat flap, followed by one paw, then another. He looked down. Something was wrong. There were feathers on the floor.

'Run, Atticus!' Michael shouted. 'Run!'

Atticus stared at the cat basket. The jewels blinked back at him. *The magpies! They had framed him!*

'Quick, Atticus, run!' Callie yelled frantically. 'Dad thinks it was you!'

Inspector Cheddar loomed towards him, hands outstretched.

Atticus gulped. Inspector Cheddar's face had gone from green to red, like a traffic light. 'Gotcha!' he hissed. 'You . . . you . . . CAT CRIMINAL!'

Terrified, Atticus tried to wriggle his way backwards out of the cat flap. But backing out of a cat flap is like reversing a car. It's much harder than going forwards. And he wasn't as skinny as he used to be. Mrs Tucker was right. He'd been eating too many sardines. He pulled in his tummy and wriggled again. It was no use! He was stuck!

Inspector Cheddar lunged at Atticus and grabbed him firmly under his armpits. He dragged Atticus into the kitchen, picked him up roughly and held him tightly under one arm.

The children watched in horror.

'AFTER ALL WE'VE DONE FOR YOU, YOU MISERABLE MOGGY!' Inspector Cheddar shouted. 'THAT IS WHAT YOU DO TO REPAY US!' He whipped a set of handcuffs out of his pocket with his free hand. He clicked one end round Atticus's neck and the other round his wrist. SNAP! 'You're under arrest, Atticus Claw,' Inspector Cheddar said.

Atticus's ears drooped.

'CHAKA-CHAKA-CHAKA-CHAKA!' From some where outside came a harsh chattering cry.

'The magpies.' Callie started to tremble. She clung on to her brother.

'They're laughing at Atticus.' Michael shivered.

18

Atticus had never been to a police station before. He didn't like it. The first thing that happened was someone took his pawprints. Then a flashlight went off in his face as someone else took his picture. Finally he was thrown into a cell.

The cell had a bench with a thin grey blanket on it. There was a bowl of water in the corner. Apart from that it was completely bare: not the sort of place a cool cat like Atticus would choose to spend the night.

Desperately he looked about for a way to escape.

There was a grille in the door at human eye level where people came and peered at him from time to time, but the mesh was too narrow for him to squeeze through and it was nailed into the wooden frame with about a thousand tacks. It would take him the rest of his nine lives to pick them out with his teeth. His molars ached at the thought of it.

The window looked more of a possibility. It was quite high up but at least it was open. The only problem was it was covered with thick iron bars. Atticus sat down and patted his tummy with his front paws. He sighed. If he couldn't get through the cat flap it wasn't very likely he would squeeze through those bars even if he *could* jump up there. It was hopeless! He was doomed to spend the rest of his life in jail. He knew he deserved it in a way, but it meant he'd never be able to take the rest of the jewellery back. He'd never make Inspector Cheddar realise that the magpies had been involved. He'd never be able to say sorry to Mrs Cheddar and Mrs Tucker. And the worst thing was, he would never see Callie and Michael again.

He crawled under the blanket and closed his eyes.

Later that evening, Inspector Cheddar was called in to see the Chief Inspector of Bigsworth.

'Great work, Cheddar!' The Chief Inspector beamed. 'I knew you'd find the culprit.'

'Thank you, sir,' Inspector Cheddar said heavily.

'To think you had him under your own roof the whole time!'

'Yes, sir.' Inspector Cheddar sighed.

'I've told the Tofflys.'

'Good.' Inspector Cheddar nodded glumly.

'And I'm pleased to say they've decided to go ahead with the antiques fair tomorrow.'

Inspector Cheddar managed a smile. That was one good thing at least – his wife still stood a chance of getting a job on *Get Rich Quick!* But it didn't make up for the fact his family hated him. The children weren't speaking to him. Mrs Cheddar refused to take his calls. And Mrs Tucker had ridden all the way back to Littleton-on-Sea Police Station on her motorbike to pour cod-liver oil in his tea. It was tough being a Police Inspector. He almost wished he was back on traffic duty.

'I suppose I should be getting up to the Hall to check the security, sir.' Inspector Cheddar made to leave the office.

'What's the point?' The Chief Inspector of Bigsworth helped himself to a chocolate biscuit. 'The burglar's behind bars. You should be out celebrating!'

Inspector Cheddar wished he could feel as cheerful about Atticus's arrest as the Chief Inspector did. For some reason though, catching the world's greatest cat burglar had left him feeling empty inside. He hated to admit it, but he'd got used to Atticus being around. The kids had been right. It *was* nice to have a pet. It made Blossom Crescent feel more like home.

'I'll just go and have a quick look anyway,' he said, putting on his cap.

'By the way, Cheddar,' the Chief Inspector said. 'Where do you think the cat's hidden the rest of the jewellery?'

Inspector Cheddar shrugged. That was a question he'd been asking himself. Only some of the stolen goods had turned up in Atticus's basket. 'I don't know, sir,' he said, 'but I'm sure we'll find it soon.'

'Make sure you do.' The Chief Inspector of Bigsworth nodded. He sat back in his chair and put his feet on the desk. He closed his eyes. 'Then we can close the case.'

At number 2 Blossom Crescent Michael and Callie were still up. They were sitting in the kitchen with Mrs Tucker. Mrs Cheddar still wasn't back.

Atticus's basket had been taken away for forensic

examination but his food and water bowls still stood on the floor beside the back door. The children stared at them gloomily.

'He didn't steal Mum's brooch,' Callie said fiercely. 'I know he didn't. He was framed!'

'The question is,' Michael said, 'how do we prove it?'

Mrs Tucker plonked two mugs of hot chocolate down on the table. 'What we need is evidence,' she said. She pulled the ironing board out of a tall cupboard and opened it with a clang.

'Maybe the magpies left some clues,' Michael suggested.

'Good thinking,' Mrs Tucker agreed. 'Let's check the kitchen for feathers.'

Callie and Michael got down on their hands and knees. 'I've found some!' Callie cried. 'Over here by the cat flap!' She held them out in her hand.

'And there's some footprints here by his food bowl!' Michael said, examining the floor carefully.

'And something smelly's been in my washing machine!' Mrs Tucker closed it with a bang. She heaved the laundry basket on to the table. Her eyes narrowed. 'Wait a minute!' she said, peeling off a pair of pants from the top of the pile. 'Those beastly birds have been in my clean knickers. There are feathers everywhere!'

Callie and Michael couldn't help giggling. Then they remembered Atticus.

'Poor Atticus,' Callie sighed. 'He must be feeling really lonely in his cell.'

'I have an idea . . .' Mrs Tucker said thoughtfully, picking up a feather and examining it. 'Tomorrow morning we're going to set Atticus free.'

'But how can we do that?' Michael said. 'Dad will be furious!'

'Not when Atticus helps us catch these meddling magpies red-footed, he won't,' Mrs Tucker said grimly.

'You mean you think they're going to try something else?' Callie gasped.

'I certainly do.' Mrs Tucker threw the knickers back into the wash. 'That's why they want Atticus out of the way – so he can't stop them. As I said, magpies are clever. They're wicked, scheming little weasels.' She shivered. 'You can bet your barracudas we haven't seen the last of them by a long way.'

'CHAKA-CHAKA-CHAKA-CHAKA!'

Around midnight Atticus was awoken by a familiar cackle.

'Jimmy!' he hissed. 'What are you doing here?'

'That's not a very nice welcome when I've flown all the way here specially to visit you.' The magpie peered down on him from between the bars on the window, his head on one side. 'Not so superior now, are you, Atticus Claw?'

Atticus snarled. 'I'm still better than you. Sneaking about in people's houses, planting false evidence – I wouldn't do that to my worst enemy.'

'Really?' Jimmy Magpie blinked. 'I'll take that as a compliment. Looks like we've overtaken you. We're the greatest BIRD burglars in the world! You're the greatest cat BUNGLER! Chaka-chaka-chaka-chaka.'

'You won't get away with it,' Atticus hissed. 'The children know you did it.'

'Not the little kiddiewinks.' Jimmy put on his baby voice. 'Ooh, I'm scared!'

'Don't talk about my friends like that.' Atticus bared his teeth. If only he could get up to the window, he'd wipe that smirk off Jimmy's beak once and for all. 'It won't be long before someone takes a look in that nest of yours and sees what you've been up to. You'll go down for years.'

'That?' Jimmy boasted. 'That's nothing compared to what we've got planned for tomorrow.'

'Tomorrow?'

'Ever heard of the Tofflys' tiara?' Jimmy whispered.

Atticus's green eyes widened. 'You're going to hit the Toffly Hall antiques fair,' he breathed.

'It was Thug and Slasher's idea,' Jimmy said generously. 'They eavesdropped when your precious Cheddars were having a little chat about it over breakfast. Then they went up to the Hall and cased the joint. I decided not to tell you about it. Just as well, as things turned out. I wasn't sure we could trust you. And it turns out I was right.'

'You lying cheat!'

'Too bad, pussy cat. Anyway, what about *you* – sucking up to those cheesy Cheddars? Moving in with them, even. You kept that pretty quiet, didn't you?'

'It was an accident. And don't talk about them like that!'

'Ah, how cute – the kitty's gone all cuddly!' Jimmy mocked. 'Can't say I blame you, though. Very cosy it is there too. I wouldn't mind paying them another visit soon.'

'Grrrrr . . .' Atticus hated Jimmy crowing about the Cheddars as though he knew them. It made his fur stand on end to think of Thug and Slasher listening in on their family conversations and the three magpies making themselves at home in Mrs Tucker's tidy kitchen. It was *his* home, not the magpies'. At least it had been.

'Keep your whiskers on, Claw,' Jimmy said. 'We won't hurt them. It's the diamonds we're after. And whatever else we can pick up at the antiques fair. I hear on the bird-vine there's going to be some nice stuff about.' He grinned. 'And now you're safely tucked up in here, the cops aren't expecting any trouble.' He cackled. 'Chaka-chaka-chaka-chaka! I'm afraid your Inspector Cheddar and his missus are in for a nasty surprise. It's traffic duty he hates, right? Well he'll be getting plenty of that after tomorrow.'

'You won't get away with it,' Atticus said fiercely. 'Three measly magpies against hundreds of humans? You don't stand a chance.'

'Who said anything about three of us?' Jimmy's eyes shone brilliantly in the moonlight. 'I've asked a few pals along. Thug and Slasher have been spreading the word. It's going to be quite a party, isn't it, lads?' He rattled his beak along the bars and flew off.

Atticus heard the rush of wings. In the moonlight

he saw a flock of birds swoop and dive across the sky. There were hundreds of magpies – thousands possibly. 'CHAKA-CHAKA-CHAKA-CHAKA!' The night was alive with the sound of excited chattering.

Atticus was beside himself. He had to get out of there! He had to warn Inspector Cheddar. He had to tell Mrs Cheddar and Callie and Michael. He threw himself at the cell door, yowling. When that didn't work he jumped on to the bench and hurled himself at the window. When that didn't work either, he curled up on the cold floor and pressed his face to the wall. If only Callie and Michael would come. If only he hadn't been so stupid.

For the first time in his life, Atticus Grammaticus Cattypuss Claw, the world's greatest cat burglar, was stumped.

1.9

Michael had always wanted a ride on a motorbike. Up until this morning he'd never been allowed. But his parents were at Toffly Hall checking everything was ready for the fair. Mrs Tucker was firm. They were going to rescue Atticus.

'Michael – you're behind me on the seat. Callie – you're in the sidecar.'

Michael pulled his helmet down tight over his ears like he did when he went go-karting and climbed on behind Mrs Tucker. Callie did the same and jumped into the sidecar.

'Hang on!' Mrs Tucker pressed the throttle. VRROOOMM! The motorbike sped down Blossom Crescent and into Townley Road. It wouldn't take them long to get to the police station.

Suddenly Mrs Tucker pulled on the brakes. The

tyres squealed as the motorbike skidded to a halt.

'What's wrong?' Michael demanded. 'Why have we stopped?'

'Look at that!' Mrs Tucker pointed to a big poster beside the railway bridge.

TOFFLY HALL ANTIQUES FAIR

SATURDAY 26 JULY

WITH RUPERT RICH AND THE GANG FROM 'GET RICH QUICK!'

ATTACK THE ATTIC, MAKE A PACKET!!!

'And now look up there.' Mrs Tucker pointed to the top of the railway bridge. Crowds of magpies jostled for space above the giant poster. Dozens more circled above.

'CHAKA-CHAKA-CHAKA-CHAKA!'

'What are they doing?' Callie asked.

'I don't know, but I've got a bad feeling.' Mrs

Tucker whipped out a pair of binoculars from her basket and gazed into the sky. A dark grey cloud loomed on the horizon. She pointed to it. 'It looks like they're moving in the direction of Toffly Hall.'

'You mean that's a cloud of *birds*?' Michael gasped in horror. He grabbed the binoculars. The cloud was moving at speed across the sky, twisting and turning like a tornado. He could just about make out that it was made up of hundreds and hundreds of magpies.

'The antiques fair!' Callie gasped.

Mrs Tucker nodded grimly. 'They'll be after the jewellery. I suspected as much. We'd better get Atticus quickly. The sight of him will make their wings wiggle!'

'Wait!' Michael swung the binoculars to the top of the railway bridge. Two magpies stood at the head of the crowd. One of them was thin with a hooked foot. The other was fat with a raggedy tail.

'It's them!' he cried, pointing. 'The magpies who tried to steal Dad's badge last week.'

Mrs Tucker narrowed her eyes. 'What about that one?' She jabbed a finger towards a huge magpie with glossy blue and green feathers that swooped and dived in front of the others, chattering wildly at the top of its voice.

Michael gazed at the bird through the binoculars. Its eyes glittered.

'That's the one who was fighting with Atticus at the pier!' he gasped.

'He's the ringleader,' Mrs Tucker yelled. 'He's the one we've got to watch! I think he's stirring them up to something big. We'd better get Atticus,' she said again. 'That bird looks tricky. Atticus is the only one who'll be able to catch him. Quick!' She snapped her visor shut. They zoomed off again on the motorbike.

At the police station, the duty sergeant was glued to the TV. He was feeling left out. All his police friends were up at Toffly Hall for the filming of *Get Rich Quick!* while he was stuck here guarding the cat burglar. And from the looks of it, they were having a whale of a time stuffing themselves with sausage rolls and nosying about in front of the TV cameras to see if anyone would hit the jackpot. It wasn't fair. The duty sergeant really wanted to go. He'd found an old metal teaspoon under the compost heap last weekend and he was sure it was worth a fortune. He sighed. He'd never be rich at this rate.

BASH! BANG! THUMP! The duty sergeant looked up in surprise. A big lady in biking leathers and two children had burst through the door of the police station. They were all wearing crash helmets.

'We're here for the cat.' Mrs Tucker flicked up her visor and thumped her basket down on the counter. 'He's wanted in connection with er . . .'

'Sardine smuggling,' Michael said quickly. 'We're from the SAS.'

'The SAS?' The duty sergeant gulped. He'd heard of them. They were a type of special soldier who could skin rabbits with their toenails. He scratched his head and peered at the children. Either he was getting old or they were recruiting them young these days.

'The Sardine Army Squadron,' Mrs Tucker snapped. 'We've come to interrogate Claw.'

The duty sergeant frowned. 'Inspector Cheddar didn't say anything about that,' he muttered, checking his logbook.

'Inspector Cheddar doesn't know.' Mrs Tucker leaned over the counter. 'This came right from the top,' she hissed. 'Our instructions come from er . . .'

'The Prime Minister!' said Callie in a muffled voice. Her helmet was stuck.

'Yeah, him,' Mrs Tucker said. 'He's very concerned about sardines, in case you didn't know. They could be in danger, thanks to Atticus Claw and his friends.'

'It's vital that we see the prisoner,' Michael said. 'Or they might become extinct.'

'And then you'd be held responsible,' Mrs Tucker added. She shook her head. 'Fish murderer is not a name I'd want.'

'Well, in that case.' The duty sergeant wavered. He felt about in his pocket for the teaspoon. He'd brought it along anyway, just in case. 'Would you mind if I popped out for a minute and left you to it?'

'Good idea.' Mrs Tucker held the door open for him. 'And don't tell a dover sole! It's HUSH HUSH.'

The duty sergeant jumped in a squad car and disappeared.

'Michael, get the keys,' Mrs Tucker ordered.

Michael grabbed the bunch of keys from a hook on the wall.

They raced to the cells.

A pitiful meowing could be heard coming from one of them.

'That's him!' Callie yelled. 'Hang on, Atticus, we're coming!'

Michael tried several keys. Finally he found one that fitted. He turned the big iron key in the lock. The cell door swung open with a creak.

'Oh, Atticus,' the children cried, tumbling inside. 'We're so glad to see you!'

Atticus looked up in amazement. He'd hardly dared hope this would happen. Yet here they were! And Mrs Tucker too – with a basket of sardines if he wasn't very much mistaken! Atticus could have cried for joy, except cats don't cry, so instead he leapt into Michael's arms and lay on his back with his paws dangling in the air so that Callie could give him a tickle. He purred throatily.

The children laughed. Even Mrs Tucker seemed pleased to see him. 'You've lost a bit of weight,' she said, fishing in her basket and producing a sardine. 'They haven't been feeding you properly. Here!'

Atticus gulped down the sardine in one. He didn't think he could ever be this happy again.

For a moment everyone forgot about the magpies.

Then the sky went dark.

'It's the cloud of birds!' Michael cried. 'It's even bigger than before!'

Atticus growled. He could see the magpies swirling about beyond the bars of the window. The sound of chattering filled the air. They were getting ready to swoop.

Mrs Tucker glanced at her watch. It was twelve-thirty. 'We haven't a moment to lose!' she cried. 'The Tofflys' tiara is being unveiled at two. She closed her basket with a snap. 'Come on, Atticus, we've got some magpies to catch.' Suddenly her eyes twinkled. 'And I know just the man to help us.'

20

Mr and Mrs Tucker lived in a row of brightly painted cottages on the seafront about half a mile from the pier. It was easy enough to guess which one was the Tuckers' because there was a rowing boat in the garden.

Mr Tucker answered the door. He was a small man with a long beard and a smelly jumper. Either that or he was a small man with a long jumper and a smelly beard. The two had somehow got mixed together as though someone had used his beard to knit his jumper. Or vice versa.

'Aha, me hearties,' he bellowed. 'I've been expecting yooze. I knew yooze was coming. I could feel it in me wooden leg!'

'Don't be silly, Herman,' Mrs Tucker said. 'I told you we'd be here before lunch. It's nothing to do with your wooden leg.' She pushed past him into the house. Atticus squeezed after her. Callie and Michael hovered on the doorstep.

'No need to be shy!' Mr Tucker bellowed. 'Come on inside.'

They followed Mr Tucker as he clunked into the house.

Mrs Tucker shooed them into the sitting room. To the children's astonishment the walls were covered with pictures of Mr Tucker wrestling with fierce-looking sea monsters. There was even one of him fighting off a giant lobster with his wooden leg.

'I keeps a camera on board me boat,' Mr Tucker explained modestly, 'to get a few snaps for me album.'

'We should show these to Dad!' Callie whispered.

'Did I ever tell you the story about how I lost me leg?' Mr Tucker unscrewed it and fell backwards into an armchair.

'No!' said Michael. 'We've never met you before.'

'Aarrhhhh, that'll be why.' Mr Tucker took his teeth out and sucked his gums. 'Let me see now. It was a dark and stormy night . . .'

'Not now, Herman,' Mrs Tucker said. 'We haven't got much time. We need to go over the plan.'

163

The children sat forward on the sofa.

Mr Tucker put his teeth back in.

Atticus hopped up on to Mr Tucker's lap. He wasn't put off by the smell coming from Mr Tucker's beard-jumper. Quite the opposite, in fact. He thought there might be a few tasty morsels lurking around in there somewhere. He started picking at it with his claws.

'Pay attention, Atticus!' Mrs Tucker snapped.

Atticus's good ear drooped. He turned round.

'The first thing we need to do is to make Atticus a disguise,' Mrs Tucker said. 'Toffly Hall will be crawling with cops.'

'Like crabs in a bucket,' Mr Tucker agreed.

' . . . If anyone sees him he'll be arrested again. Atticus, your job will be to go after the ringleader and his two sidekicks. They're our main target. Is that okay?'

'Grrrrr,' Atticus growled. It would be his pleasure.

'Good.' Mrs Tucker pursed her lips. 'Once we've caught them, with any luck the rest of those bothersome birds will take off. If they don't, that's where Michael and Callie come in. And you, Herman. Did you get everything ready like I told you?'

'I's got me nets . . .' Mr Tucker lit a pipe. The room filled with blue smoke.

Michael and Callie started coughing.

' . . . And me lobster pots. And me lines. And me hooks. And me bucket. And me rope. They're all strapped on to me trailer.'

Mrs Tucker nodded approvingly. 'What about the worms?'

Mr Tucker patted his pockets. 'In me trousers,' he confirmed. 'Hundreds of them, all wriggling around like eels.' He took a quick puff on his pipe.

'I'm guessing the boss magpie and his mates will go for the Tofflys' tiara and the rest of them will grab what they can,' Mrs Tucker said. 'Atticus, you and I will take out the BIG THREE and get them into pots. Michael and Callie, you wait with Mr Tucker until we give the signal. If the rest don't fly away, the plan is to capture the birds when they swoop on the other antiques. Mr Tucker will throw down some worms for good measure and – BHAM! – you move in with the nets. Got it?'

The children nodded.

'Will Mum be in danger?' Michael asked in a worried voice. 'She's in charge of the tiara.'

'No, I don't think the magpies will hurt anyone,'

Mrs Tucker reassured him. 'They just want the loot.'

Atticus hoped she was right. Jimmy Magpie had promised no one would get hurt but would he stick to his word? If things got nasty, there was no telling what the horrible bird might do. Atticus was glad he was going to be there – no bird-brained magpie would hurt Mrs Cheddar or the kids with him there to protect them.

Atticus purred reassuringly to let Michael and Callie know he had it covered.

'How are you going to get close enough to the tiara?' Callie asked. 'Loads of people will be there. Mum said they were expecting huge crowds, especially when Rupert Rich tells the *Get Rich Quick!* viewers how much he thinks the tiara's worth.'

'I've thought of that,' Mrs Tucker said. 'I'm going to pretend I've got something even more valuable than the Tofflys' tiara to show Rupert Rich. When he starts doing his "Attack the attic, make a packet!" routine, that's when I'll show up with *my* ruby necklace.'

'You've got a ruby necklace?' Mr Tucker bellowed. 'Why didn't you say so?'

'It's not real, you silly old fishfinger!' Mrs Tucker said, exasperated. 'Otherwise I'd be living at Toffly Hall myself! I've got a fake one that belonged to my grandmother. It's made of glass but it'll fool everyone long enough for us to snatch the magpies.'

'But what if Dad sees you?' Michael said. 'He might not let you near Rupert Rich. He'll guess it's not real.'

'That's the best part!' Mrs Tucker chortled. 'I'm not going as Mrs Edna Tucker – feisty fishwife from Littleton-on-Sea; I'm going as Countess Salmonella Von Troutperch – loaded lady with lots of lolly from Los Angeles. I'll pretend I've come over specially for the show with my perfect Persian cat.' She shot a look at Atticus.

Persian cat?! Atticus thought. *Where was she going to get one of those at such short notice?*

'Brilliant!' bellowed Mr Tucker, banging his leg on the table. 'You'll look smashing in rubies.'

'Oh, *I'm* not wearing them,' Mrs Tucker said.

Mr Tucker, Callie and Michael stared at her, puzzled.

'Who is, then?'

Mrs Tucker grinned. 'Atticus.' She folded her arms. 'We're going to dye him white.'

21

Michael and Mr Tucker dragged a reluctant Atticus into the bathroom while Mrs Tucker went with Callie to get changed.

The bathroom was full of bottles of different shapes and sizes.

Atticus eyed them warily.

'What are all these for?' Michael asked, staring at the forest of multi-coloured glass.

'I'll tell yooze.' Mr Tucker tapped a few with the stick of his pipe. The glass made a tune. Next he started banging his wooden leg on the tile floor. Soon he had a rhythm going. He cleared his throat noisily. Suddenly, to Atticus's astonishment, he broke into a sea shanty.

'*Once upon a time when men were fish,*' he sang,

'*They all ate each other and then went squish,*

One of them invented eyeball oil, Just put it in a pan and let it boil . . .'

Michael giggled.

Atticus put his paws over his ears. He'd heard donkeys with tonsillitis sing better than that.

'HERE COMES THE CHORUS!' Mr Tucker yelled. 'JOIN IN IF YOU LIKE!'

'*This one makes you hairy,*' he bellowed, tapping away at the glass, '*this one makes you smaaarrrt,*' he banged his leg on the floor, '*this one cures verrucas,*

And this one makes you faarrrt.'

'You'd better not get them mixed up,' Atticus growled.

'*This one makes you smelly,*' Mr Tucker yodelled, '*This one makes you moo, This one helps your hearing, And this one makes you poo!'*

Michael was laughing his head off.

Atticus couldn't understand why. There was nothing funny about it. Mr Tucker was bonkers. He was one scale short of a fish skin. He was mad, barmy, doolally and dangerous. There was no knowing what was in those bottles. Michael wouldn't be laughing if one of them were about to get tipped all over *him*! This was serious. Atticus might turn into a cow or start farting or both. And he definitely didn't have verrucas. Atticus felt so worried he thought he might faint.

'Aaarrrr, here's what we's lookin' fooorrrrr!' Mr Tucker stopped singing suddenly and picked up a heavy green bottle with a blue label and a thick rubber stopper.

Atticus stared at the label in disbelief.

THUMPERS'

Traditional White Beard Dye
Puts years on you in an instant.
Strongly recommended by sailors.
(Can Also Be Used on Jumpers)

No . . . no . . . no . . . no . . . NO!!!! Before Atticus could jump away, Mr Tucker had bundled him into the bath, whisked off his red handkerchief and lathered him all over with Thumpers' Traditional White.

'It says on the label you have to leave it on for an hour to set,' Michael said anxiously.

An hour! Stuck in the bath with this gunk all over him? Atticus didn't think so. He got ready to spring.

'We don't have an hour,' Mr Tucker grunted. 'We'll just have to hope it laaarsts long enough to catch them magpies. Rinse him off would you, Michael?'

Rinse him off??!! Didn't they know cats hated water? Atticus panicked. He tried to scramble out of the bath but his feet kept slipping on the soapy white bubbles.

'Sorry, Atticus!' Michael started the shower. 'I know you don't like it, but you've got to let me do this.'

'I've got him!' Mr Tucker's big hands closed round Atticus's body.

Atticus wriggled helplessly. He heard a hiss then a gurgle. Suddenly he was hit by a deluge of water. *Were they trying to kill him?!* He was drowning! He couldn't breathe! His fur was being matted and mangled! Even his chewed ear was soggy!

'Careful it doesn't go in his eyes,' Mr Tucker remarked. 'That stuff will sting like a jellyfish!'

'I'm being as careful as I can,' Michael complained. 'Stop wriggling, Atticus, it's just water!'

Just water?! How could humans say that? It was torture. It was cat cruelty. It would give him nightmares for years. Atticus screwed his eyes shut and let out a pitiful yowl.

'There,' Michael said eventually. 'You're done.'

Atticus stopped yowling. He opened his eyes cautiously. He was still alive – just – but freezing cold. He began to shiver.

'Now, let's get you blow-dried.' Mr Tucker scooped Atticus up in a towel and took him through to the bedroom. 'Then we'll show the ladies.'

Being blow-dried was much better than being dyed. Atticus closed his eyes as the warm stream of air fluffed out his fur. It was like being tickled. The only off-putting thing was the noise. Someone should invent a hairdryer that didn't scream.

'Wow,' Michael whispered solemnly when he'd finished. 'You look completely different, Atticus.'

Atticus swallowed. *Completely different*. It didn't sound like Michael meant it in a good way.

'Have a look in the mirror,' Mr Tucker encouraged.

Atticus padded over to the dressing table and

hopped up on to the stool. He stared. A strange-looking cat with white fluffy fur and a chewed ear stared back at him.

Atticus blinked.

The cat in the mirror blinked back.

Atticus put out a paw.

So did the cat in the mirror.

It really is me, he thought. *That's weird.*

'Don't worry, Atticus,' Mr Tucker said. 'It won't laaarrrst very long.' He made a slurping noise with his false teeth. 'And mind yooze don't lick it off.'

Yuk! Don't worry, he wouldn't. Atticus was glad the dye would wear off quickly though. He didn't mind being a Persian cat for a few hours but he didn't want to stay like that for the rest of his life. White made him look a bit of a sissy.

'Atticus!' Callie ran into the bedroom. 'Is that really you? You look even more handsome than usual!'

Atticus purred modestly. Perhaps white suited him after all.

'Huh-hum!' A cough came from the doorway.

'Oh, sorry!' Callie made a little bow. 'May I present Countess Salmonella Von Troutperch?'

Mrs Tucker waltzed into the room in a long puffy

173

purple dress. She had a black shawl around her shoulders and a blonde curly wig on her head. 'Darlings!' she said in a posh American accent. 'How perfectly peachy to perceive you!'

'Edna, you look like a million dollars,' Mr Tucker gasped. 'I'd never have recognised yooze.'

Mrs Tucker grinned at Atticus. 'And you look like you've seen a ghost! I wouldn't have known you apart from the chewed ear,' she chortled. 'Let's hope the magpies don't notice it. Here, get these on.' She fastened the fake ruby choker around Atticus's neck and swept him up in her arms.

Mr Tucker whistled. 'Make that two million dollars! You sure it's glass?'

'Supremely certain, darling,' Mrs Tucker said in her posh voice.

The children clapped their hands in delight. No one would ever know it was Mrs Tucker. Or Atticus – as long as the dye didn't rub off!

Mrs Tucker and Atticus admired their reflections in the mirror for a few seconds. Then Mrs Tucker raced to the stairs and took them two at a time. 'Come on, everyone,' she cried. 'What are we waiting for? LET'S CATCH SOME CROOKS!'

22

Up at Toffly Hall the antiques fair was in full swing. Most of the stalls were inside the great marquee. Queues of people were waiting patiently to see if they would make a packet. So far, though, nothing very exciting had happened.

Lord and Lady Toffly were talking to the Chief Inspector of Bigsworth by the marquee entrance.

'So I told Mrs Cheddar to get the men to put it on the south-south-south west-west-west lawn in the end,' Lady Toffly explained. 'That way it doesn't spoil the view from the library *or* ruin the begonias.'

'Bravo, Antonia,' said Lord Toffly. 'Thank goodness someone's got some sense around here. That Cheddar woman's so dippy – like the cheese you get in Switzerland.'

'And it's right next to the rose garden, which is

where Rupert Rich wants to value my tiara,' Lady Toffly remarked.

'It's worth trillions, you know,' Lord Toffly boasted. 'Zillions, probably.'

'Rupert says he needs natural light,' Lady Toffly explained, 'so that he can tell us exactly how many carrots it is.'

'Carats.' The Chief Inspector of Bigsworth stifled a yawn. 'Not carrots. They're the things rabbits eat.'

'Rabbits?' Lord Toffly sounded puzzled. 'Eating diamonds? What an extraordinary thing. The police should do something about it, Chief Inspector.'

'Talking of the police, how's that Gorgonzola fellow?' Lady Toffly asked. 'I must say I was pleased when he caught that hedgehog.'

'It was a cat,' the Chief Inspector told her. 'Not a hedgehog.'

'Really?' Lord Toffly looked startled. 'Are you sure? I've seen some dodgy-looking hedgehogs in my time. They look pretty tricky to me.'

The Chief Inspector of Bigsworth felt like shouting 'Don't be an idiot' at Lord Toffly, like he did at most of his police officers when they said something stupid. Luckily he remembered just in time that Lord and Lady Toffly were very, very rich and he needed donations for the Police Helmets Fund. He clamped his mouth shut.

Just then a man with big hair, a bright green jacket and an orange suntan rushed over, accompanied by Mrs Cheddar. A crew of cameramen jogged behind them. Inspector Cheddar jogged behind *them*.

'Rupert!' Lady Toffly exclaimed. 'Are you ready to talk tiara turkey?'

'Rupe, old man!' Lord Toffly thumped him on the back. 'Hope you've got your calculator ready with loads of noughts on!'

Rupert Rich flashed his teeth. It wasn't really a smile. More like a row of piano keys. 'Yeah,' he said. 'I've been looking forward to seeing this baby all day. Do you know what a lot of rotten old rubbish people bring in? I had one guy with a teaspoon he'd found on the compost heap. I told him it cost 20p from the Co-op. He seemed really upset. Good TV though. Makes for a great show, especially when you know you've got the biggy to look forward to at the end.' He flashed his teeth at Mrs Cheddar. 'It's been brilliantly organised so far, I must say.'

'Thanks!' Mrs Cheddar smiled back.

'Biggy!' Lord Toffly exclaimed. 'This is a hugey! It's an enormousy! It's the size of a housey!'

Inspector Cheddar tried to squeeze his wife's hand. 'Congratulations, darling,' he whispered. 'Everything's going according to plan!'

Mrs Cheddar scowled at him. '*Your* plan, maybe!' she hissed. 'To get rid of Atticus.'

Inspector Cheddar sighed. Not that again!

'But I don't think it was just Atticus who burgled those houses,' Mrs Cheddar muttered. 'You should have listened to what the children said about the magpies . . .'

'Yeah, well, I think we should get on with the show.' Rupert Rich glanced at the sky. 'A few clouds are gathering. We don't want to get rained on. It'll spoil my hair. And I'm keen to do the valuation outside like we agreed. I want a shot of me against the yellow roses – they'll look good with my jacket. GOT THAT?' he yelled at the camera crew.

Everyone jumped.

Rupert Rich turned to the Tofflys and rubbed his hands together. 'Time to "attack the attic and make a packet!"' He strode off towards the rose garden.

The camera crew picked up their equipment and jogged after him.

'See you later.' Mrs Cheddar gave her husband a dirty look and trotted after *them*.

The Tofflys skipped off in the other direction – hand in hand towards the Hall.

'Shouldn't I get some of my officers to go with them?' Inspector Cheddar asked the Chief Inspector of Bigsworth anxiously.

'Relax, Cheddar,' the Chief Inspector snapped. 'You worry too much. The cat's behind bars. Nothing can go wrong now.'

'Inspector Cheddar?' A young woman rushed up to him. She had beautiful long dark hair and a flowery top. 'I've got something important to tell you.'

'Miss Rana!' Inspector Cheddar greeted her with a cheerful smile. 'We hope to have some news on your missing emeralds soon.'

The woman shook her head impatiently. 'No, you don't understand. I found them! They turned up in my handbag. I honestly don't know how they got there. I was sure they were in the safe.' She went off to join a friend.

Inspector Cheddar stared after her. It was then that he heard a strange noise.

'CHAKA-CHAKA-CHAKA-CHAKA.'

He glanced up sharply. It was coming from somewhere in the rose garden where Rupert Rich was heading with Mrs Cheddar and the TV team. He listened closely.

'Chaka-chaka-chaka-chaka!'

The noise came again, quieter this time. It was followed by a thump and a loud SQUAWK.

Inspector Cheddar frowned. What a weird sound! Chatter-chatter-chatter! It was as though someone was laughing at them.

Suddenly Inspector Cheddar's eyes started popping. His face went red. *Chattering?! Laughing?!! Emeralds in handbags?!!!*

Atticus *wasn't* the burglar. At least not the only one! Everything Callie and Michael had said was true. Atticus had been trying to say sorry. He had put the emeralds back. The magpies had framed him. Now they were after the Tofflys' tiara! His wife had been right!

He glanced up at the sky. The clouds were moving quickly towards the Hall. They swirled and swished around. He peered closer.

'Oh my giddy aunt!' he said. His face went from red to purple. His mouth opened and closed like a fish.

'What's the matter, Cheddar?' The Chief Inspector was looking at him with concern. 'You look like you've swallowed a noodle the wrong way.'

Inspector Cheddar's teeth chattered. 'I...I... I . . . think we're in for a storm, sir.'

He galloped off towards the Hall.

'Where are you going now?' the Chief Inspector yelled.

'I'm going to check on the Tofflys,' Inspector Cheddar yelled back. 'Just in case.'

Just at that moment the Tuckers zoomed into the car park in a cloud of dust. Atticus squeezed out of the sidecar where he'd been riding with Callie. Mrs Tucker had wrapped him in an old apron to keep him clean. He examined his legs and tummy and back – the bits that he could see by twisting his head. They were all still dazzlingly white. He'd pass for Persian for the time being anyway. As long as the dye didn't rub off before he found Jimmy.

Mr Tucker rolled off the trailer and hoisted the fishing nets over his shoulder. 'Take these.' He gave a lobster pot each to Callie and Michael and grabbed the rope and bucket.

'Let's go!' Mrs Tucker took off her helmet and straightened her wig. 'Come on, Atticus . . . I mean Claude.'

Claude?! Atticus looked at her incredulously. Couldn't she come up with a better name than *Claude?*

'He doesn't like it,' Callie said.

'How about Henry?' Michael suggested. 'After Henry VIII?'

'He's certainly fat enough,' Mrs Tucker said. 'After all those sardines. Come along, Henry.' She scooped him up and glanced at the sky. The sound of chattering birds was getting closer. So were the clouds. 'Let's get this antiques show on the road.'

They hurried along the path towards the marquee, Mr Tucker clunking along at the rear.

'ATTENTION, ATTENTION! WOULD EVERYONE WHO WISHES TO VIEW THE TOFFLYS' TIARA, PLEASE MOVE TOWARDS THE ROSE GARDEN.'

'It's Mum!' cried Callie.

'Quick!' Michael yelled. 'It's nearly time.'

'I can't go any faster!' Mr Tucker grumbled. 'Me leg'll fall off.'

'ATTENTION, ATTENTION, WOULD EVERYONE WHO WANTS TO SEE ME LOOKING HANDSOME AND MAYBE GET ON THE TELLY PLEASE GET A MOVE ON.'

182

'It's Rupert Rich!' Mrs Tucker gasped. 'He's about to do the valuation. Sorry, Herman, but you'll have to catch us up.' She chased along the path clutching Atticus, Callie and Michael in hot pursuit.

They reached the entrance to the rose garden. Hundreds of people were pushing and shoving their way forwards. They were all carrying the things they had brought to be valued. Some people were wearing jewellery; others had watches and trinkets stuffed into bags. The duty sergeant pushed past with a teaspoon protruding from his pocket. No one was paying much attention to their own antiques because they were all in such a rush to see Rupert Rich and the Tofflys' tiara.

They would make easy pickings for the magpies.

'This way!' Mrs Tucker raced round the outside of the walled garden.

Careful! Atticus bounced up and down in her arms. He was beginning to feel quite sick. It was like being on Mr Tucker's boat in a hurricane!

Luckily there was another gate and it was unlocked. Mrs Tucker lifted the latch and peered in. The gate opened on to an area of the rose garden that had been cordoned off from the crowds. Rupert Rich was sitting at a table on a stage in front of a bed of yellow roses. Before him was a bank of cameras and behind them, on the lawn, was the crowd. Next to Rupert Rich sat the Tofflys with Mrs Cheddar. A little way away, on the path, Inspector Cheddar paced up and down practising karate chops.

'There it is!' Michael whispered. The table was covered with a red velvet cloth. Propped up on the cloth was a battered leather jewellery case marked TOFFLYS' TIARA – KEEP OFF.

'Are we rolling?' Rupert Rich asked the camera crew.

Someone answered by snapping a clapperboard.

Rupert Rich flashed his teeth at the crowd. 'Welcome again to *Get Rich Quick!*,' he cried.

Everyone cheered.

'There hasn't been much to shout about so far today, but we've had a few nice things to look at, so well done everyone who didn't bring in mouldy tea-spoons from the compost heap!'

The duty sergeant blushed.

'Now for the part you've all been waiting for.' Rupert Rich paused. 'The Tofflys' tiara.'

'*Attack the attic and make a packet!*' The crowd chanted.

'Chaka-chaka-chaka-chaka!'

'It's the magpies!' Michael whispered.

Mrs Tucker was still trying to get her breath back. 'I feel like a cod on a fish hook,' she complained. 'And my wig's slipped. But I'll just have to do. Callie and Michael: you wait here for Mr Tucker. We'll try and hold them off until he gets here. Come on, Atticus.' She strolled into the garden.

Atticus lay snugly in her arms, trying to look regal and Henry the Eighth-ish.

'May I?' Rupert Rich produced an eyeglass from his pocket and squeezed it into his right eye. He reached for the Tofflys' leather jewellery case and opened it.

'Ooooohhhhh!' The crowd gasped.

The fabulous tiara glittered and shone.

'Chaka-chaka-chaka-chaka!'

'Oh no!' Michael glanced round. 'We need to hurry. Where's Mr Tucker?'

'Oi! Hang on a minute!'

Rupert Rich looked up. A large lady with lopsided blonde hair and a puffy purple dress was making her way on to the stage carrying a large white cat.

'Who are you?' he asked.

'I, my good man, am Countess Salmonella Von Troutperch,' Mrs Tucker said haughtily, remembering just in time to put on her posh American voice.

'Go away!' said Lady Toffly.

'You're not invited,' agreed Lord Toffly.

Mrs Tucker ignored them. 'I have about my cat's person something very valuable that I'd like you to take a look at.' She stroked Atticus around the neck. 'My dear grandmother's ruby necklace.'

'Aaaahhhh,' the crowd gasped as the cameras panned in on Atticus.

'Who *was* your grandmother?' Lady Toffly asked suspiciously.

'I've never heard of the Von Troutperches,' Lord Toffly complained.

'She was the Duchess of Seabass,' Mrs Tucker said without hesitation. 'It's a small island off Cornwall. She lost all her money in the great herring famine of 1920 and sailed to Cape Cod in a tin bath.'

'Let's have a look then.' Rupert Rich was enjoying himself. This was going to make great TV. His ratings would go through the roof. 'Get 'em off the cat.'

'Certainly not!' Mrs Tucker said. 'Henry never goes anywhere without his ruby collar, do you, Henry?'

Atticus purred complacently. It was fun pretending to be a posh Persian.

'Put him down next to the tiara, then,' Rupert Rich said, 'so I can take a look at them both.'

186

Mrs Tucker placed Atticus on the table and stepped away from the stage. She winked at him. He was in a perfect position now for when the magpies struck.

Rupert Rich squinted through his eyeglass at the fake rubies. Then he squinted at the Tofflys' tiara. Then he did the same again.

The crowd held its breath.

'It's getting awfully dark,' Rupert Rich complained. 'I can hardly see a thing.'

Clouds were gathering in the sky.

Mrs Tucker had joined the children at the gate.

'The magpies!' whispered Callie. 'They're here.'

23

'CHAKA-CHAKA-CHAKA-CHAKA!'

'CHAKA-CHAKA-CHAKA-CHAKA!'

All of a sudden the birds swooped.

There was pandemonium.

The crowd was packed in tight. There was no-where to run. The only thing to do was duck as the magpies descended on the rose garden.

'Keep filming!' Rupert Rich shrieked, sliding off his chair and hiding under the table.

The cameras rolled as swarms of beady-eyed birds fluttered and pecked at the lovely glittery things all the people had brought to the antiques fair.

'Don't panic!' shouted Inspector Cheddar, trying out a few karate kicks. 'They won't hurt you. They're only after your jewellery!' WHACK! 'Oops, sorry, sir!' He realised, too late, he had bashed the Chief

Inspector of Bigsworth on the bum by mistake.

'Cheddar!' the Chief Inspector roared. 'You're on traffic cones for the rest of your career!'

'Yes, sir.' Inspector Cheddar didn't care any more. All he wanted was to help his wife save the Tofflys' tiara before the magpies got it. Otherwise she'd never be asked to organise anything ever again and it would be all his fault. He should have listened to her! He started to fight his way through the milling crowd towards the stage.

Up on the stage the Tofflys were frozen with terror.

'I knew it!' Mrs Cheddar grabbed the tiara. Atticus threw himself in front of her, yowling at the top of his voice. If Jimmy and his gang tried to steal it, they'd have to get past him first.

Mrs Cheddar stared at his chewed ear. 'Atticus?' she said.

Quickly, Atticus licked a patch of fur on his leg so she could see his real colour underneath. 'PPTHTHPPHTT!' Mr Tucker's Thumpers' Beard Dye tasted disgusting. He spat it out on Lady Toffly by mistake. Her eyebrows went white.

'Atticus, it really is you!' Mrs Cheddar cried. 'Oh,

I'm so happy you're here. I knew all along that those mangy magpies were mostly to blame!'

'CHAKA-CHAKA-CHAKA-CHAKA!' Two magpies landed awkwardly on the table. One was thin with a hooked foot; the other was fat with a raggedy tail.

'Who's she calling mangy?' Thug said menacingly, advancing towards Mrs Cheddar. The tiara twinkled tantalisingly in her hand.

'The wimpy white thing in front of her, I should think,' Slasher cawed, sidling up beside Thug and giving his friend a crafty look. 'The one that looks like a soppy snowflake.'

They hopped forwards.

'Atticus, do something!' Mrs Cheddar clutched the tiara.

Atticus . . . ?

Thug and Slasher gazed at the white Persian.

'He's got a chewed ear,' Thug gulped, his knees knocking.

'You don't think . . . I mean it can't be . . . *Claw*, can it?' Slasher trembled, his beak twitching.

'It certainly can.' Atticus grinned, showing them his sharp teeth. 'Nice to see you, boys. By the way, Slasher, who are you calling a wimp? Only I find that quite offensive coming from a cowardly crow like you.' He pounced on the birds and pinned them by the tail.

'Aaarrrghghh!' screamed Slasher, struggling to get free. 'Don't eat me!'

'Heeellllpppp!' sobbed Thug, lying flat on his tummy on the velvet tablecloth and covering his eyes with his wings. 'I'm too young to die.'

Mrs Tucker hurled a lobster pot over the crowd. It landed with a thump on the table. 'Bung 'em in there, Atticus,' she yelled. 'I'm going to help Mr Tucker. He must have got his leg stuck in a drain.'

Atticus tossed the two birds into the lobster pot and snapped the door shut.

'Mr Tucker's here?' Inspector Cheddar crawled on to the stage. He'd had a nasty experience with one magpie that kept trying to hit him in the eye with a teaspoon.

'And Atticus!' Mrs Cheddar cried.

'And the children.' Mrs Tucker screeched.

Inspector Cheddar grabbed a microphone. 'Don't worry!' he gasped. 'Everything's under control. The police have it covered!' He took the Tofflys' tiara from Mrs Cheddar and held it up for everyone to see. 'Rest assured, whatever happens, no one's going to steal this!'

'Keep filming!' Rupert Rich's voice came from

under the table. 'Tell me when it's safe to come out!'

'CHAKA-CHAKA-CHAKA-CHAKA!' The evil chattering reverberated around the rose garden. The magpies were excited about something. They stopped what they were doing and looked up at the sky with gleaming eyes, jewellery dripping from their beaks.

Sounds like Inspector Cheddar spoke too soon, thought Atticus. *I wonder what's going on now?*

Just then he heard the beat of wings.

'Watch out!' he yowled.

It was too late.

Jimmy Magpie swooped down from the sky and snatched the tiara out of Inspector Cheddar's out-stretched hand.

'CHAKA-CHAKA-CHAKA-CHAKA!' Jimmy landed on top of the wall behind the stage. He placed the tiara carefully over one wing and held it aloft. The magpies chattered wildly.

The crowd watched the huge magpie, astonished. They knew it couldn't really be happening, but it looked as if he was about to make a speech!

'This is a great day for magpies,' Jimmy cawed.

'Chaka-chaka-chaka-chaka!' the magpies chattered back.

'This is the day we've all been waiting for. This is

192

the day we lay the memory of Beaky, Goon and Penguin to rest.'

The magpies all placed one wing across their breasts and muttered a little prayer.

'THIS IS THE DAY WE MAGPIES PROVE WE ARE CLEVERER THAN HUMANS!!'

The magpies swaggered about, showing off their loot.

'You might be cleverer than most humans, Jimmy,' Atticus growled, 'but you're not cleverer than Michael and Callie and their mum. You're not cleverer than Mr and Mrs Tucker. And you're certainly not cleverer than me.' He jumped down off the stage and wriggled on his belly towards the wall.

Mrs Tucker had finally managed to pull Mr Tucker's wooden leg out of the drain. The children were ready for action.

They watched as Mr Tucker emptied the contents of his trouser pockets into a large plastic bucket. The worms wriggled and squirmed, trying to get out.

Mr Tucker chuckled. 'Magpies go mad for worms, you maarrrk my woorrrds.'

Next he retrieved the long length of rope. He tied

the two ends together in a special fisherman's knot and threw the loop over a sturdy branch of a big oak tree. Testing the knot first, he tied one end of the rope securely to the handle of the bucket.

The children watched, fascinated.

'That should do it!' he said, jumping into the bucket. 'Edna, you and the kids pull on this end. READY, STEADY, HEAVE!!'

Michael and Callie pulled on the rope. Mrs Tucker pulled behind them. It was like a tug of war only at the other end of the rope wasn't another team but Mr Tucker sitting in a bucket of worms.

'Put your backs into it!' Mr Tucker shouted.

The bucket took off.

Mr Tucker sailed into the air. When he got near enough, he hopped out on to the branch of the tree and untied the bucket from the other end of the rope.

'Be careful, Herman!' Mrs Tucker called.

'Stop fussing, Edna. I've been in worse scrapes than this,' Mr Tucker grumbled. He slithered along the branch with the bucket until he was over the rose garden.

'Here goes,' he said. He stuck his hand into the bucket and began to scatter the worms.

The Chief Inspector of Bigsworth was having the worst day of his life. First he'd had to talk to the Tofflys. Then he'd been caught in a crowd of greedy antique hunters. After that he'd been besieged by a gang of ruffian magpies trying to steal his watch. Finally he'd been kicked in the bum by Inspector Cheddar. Nothing could make this evil day any fouler than it already was.

He struggled to feet.

SPLAT!

PHUT! PHUT!

SPLAT!

Something squishy landed on his bald head. He put his hand up to wipe his face and picked off something brown and squashy. The Chief Inspector sighed. 'Now it's raining worms,' he muttered.

Wait a minute. What had he just said?! He stared at the creature in his hand. RAINING WORMS!! The Chief Inspector gazed upwards. SPLODGE! A slug bounced off his cheek.

SPLAT!

PHUT! PHUT!

SPLAT!

Everyone in the crowd, including the Chief Inspector of Bigsworth, covered their faces and began to scream.

195

'Bull's eye!' Mr Tucker wriggled along the branch, re-tied the knot and jumped back in the bucket. 'Give me some slack!'

Carefully, the children and Mrs Tucker let out the rope and began to lower him down.

Soon Mr Tucker landed back at the gate.

'Good work, crew!' He stroked his beard-jumper. 'Now let's catch those creeps!' He hauled a fishing net out from the shrubbery. 'Yooze take this end.' Callie and Michael took a corner each. The net was heavy and bulky but Mr Tucker had folded it carefully so that they could spread it over the magpies easily. 'We'll take the other.'

'Look,' Michael hissed. 'There's Atticus. He's going after the ringleader.'

They watched as Atticus placed a front paw at the bottom of the wall and began to heave himself up the trellis.

'Come on,' Mrs Tucker whispered. 'We need to hurry. Before those pesky birds realise what's happening.'

24

'THREE CHEERS FOR THE MAGPIES!'

Jimmy Magpie was still in full cry when the worms landed in the rose garden. At first he didn't notice anything was wrong. He strutted up and down the wall with the tiara over his wing. 'HIP HIP . . .'

To his surprise none of his magpie audience said HOORAY. They were chattering rudely about something else.

'I said HIP HIP . . .'

The magpies paid no attention.

SPLAT!

PHUT! PHUT!

SPLAT!

Jimmy looked up. He saw a strange-looking human with a long beard and a short jumper (or the other way round) sitting in a tree scattering handfuls of worms over *his* magpie army. What was he doing?

HOP!

PECK! PECK!

HOP!

Suddenly Jimmy realised what was happening.

'NO!' he screeched.

SPLAT!

PHUT! PHUT!

SPLAT!

'Stop it!' he yelled.

HOP!

PECK! PECK!

HOP!

'Can't you see it's a trick!' he squawked.

The magpies ignored him. One by one they dropped the stolen trinkets and turned their attention to the worms.

'NOOOOOOOOO!!!!' Jimmy shrieked. 'You need to leave. Now! Scarper! Shoo! The humans are up to something!'

Some of the birds looked up in alarm and flew away.

'Chaka-chaka-chaka-chaka!' The rest of the magpies didn't pay any attention. They were too busy fighting over the worms.

 198

Suddenly the same strange-looking human who had been sitting in the tree a few minutes earlier hobbled through a gate into the rose garden. Jimmy watched in disbelief. He was with the woman in the purple dress who called herself Countess Salmonella Von Troutperch. They were closely followed by two children.

Jimmy blinked. 'The Cheddar kids!' he hissed. 'I might have known.'

'GET OUT OF THE WAY!' the countess yelled at the crowd.

Jimmy put his head on one side, puzzled. The countess didn't sound very posh now. And where was that white cat of hers?

Everyone, including the Chief Inspector of Bigsworth, crawled to the sides of the rose garden and collapsed in the flowerbeds. Some managed to struggle out of the entrance. The only creatures still on the grass were the magpies, jostling over the feast of worms.

Michael and Mrs Tucker ran to the other side of the lawn, stretching the net tight. Callie and Mr Tucker stood by the gate.

'Ready?' Mrs Tucker yelled.

'Ready!'

Holding the corners of the net tightly in their hands, Callie and Michael ran down each side of the lawn. The net flopped open behind them over the squabbling birds.

'Hold steady!' Mr Tucker warned, gripping his corner of the net in his hairy fists.

'I am, you old roach!' Mrs Tucker gripped hers.

Jimmy Magpie watched in horror.

'NOOOOOOOOOO!!' he screeched.

'OKAY! DROP IT!' Mr Tucker shouted.

FLUMP! The net landed on top of the remaining magpies.

SQUAWK! The magpies struggled and flapped. Their wings got tangled in the net. It was impossible to escape. They were trapped

'Bravo!' Inspector Cheddar yelled, racing round the net and hugging the kids.

'You were brilliant!' Mrs Cheddar ran after him and kissed the tops of their heads.

'Is it safe to come out yet?' Rupert Rich called from under the table.

'CHAKA-CHAKA-CHAKA-CHAKA!' Suddenly there was a violent chattering from the top of the wall.

'It's the ringleader!' Michael gasped. 'He's still got the tiara.'

Not for long, he hasn't! Atticus hauled himself up the last bricks. He tiptoed along the wall towards Jimmy.

'Watch out, Boss!' Thug's voice came from inside the lobster pot. 'There's a cat behind you!'

'It's Claw!' Slasher yelled.

Jimmy turned. He stared at Atticus in disbelief. 'Claw?' he repeated. 'You're supposed to be in jail.'

'No, Jimmy.' Atticus snarled. '*You are.*' He pounced.

Jimmy spread his wings to fly away but the tiara was still balanced over one of them. It was heavy. He flapped furiously with the other wing but it didn't give him enough thrust to take off. He was like an aeroplane with one engine, leaning dangerously to the side.

'Gotcha!' Atticus pinned him by the tail. But Jimmy was strong. He twisted his neck and pecked at Atticus viciously with his sharp beak. 'Ouch!' Atticus drew back. He tasted blood on his lip.

'You pathetic pampered pet,' Jimmy cackled. 'I always knew you'd turn out to be a loser. Just like a cat to wimp out of a fight.' He took hold of the tiara in his beak.

Atticus sprang forward and caught Jimmy's foot in his mouth.

Jimmy tried desperately to kick him off.

The two of them teetered on the edge of the wall.

'DO SOMETHING, DAD!' Michael shouted. 'Atticus is going to fall!'

Inspector Cheddar didn't hesitate. He sprinted back down the path in Olympic-qualifying time. 'I'm coming, Atticus!'

He reached the stage.

With one final effort, Jimmy Magpie launched himself into the air.

Atticus hung on grimly, his mouth round Jimmy's leg. *He wasn't going to let him go after everything he'd done!* He closed his eyes as they plummeted to the ground together.

'CHAKA-CHAKA-CHAKA-CHAKA!'

Jimmy let out one last despairing burst of chatter.

The tiara fell from his beak.

In one swift movement, Inspector Cheddar whipped the velvet cloth off the table and held it out in his arms.

THWUMP! Atticus and Jimmy landed in a tangle of velvet, feathers and fur.

SMASH! The tiara landed on the bare wooden

table and shattered into thousands of pieces.

There was a ghastly silence.

'Whoops!' Inspector Cheddar said.

'What have you done, you moron!' screeched Lady Toffly.

'You're a disgrace to the police force!' yelled Lord Toffly. 'You should be out arresting hedgehogs not going round breaking people's priceless hairlooms.'

'It's *heir*looms.' Rupert Rich clambered out from under the table. 'And it's not priceless. I thought as much when I was inspecting it earlier.' He flicked at the bits of crystal. 'It's glass.'

'Glass?' Lady Toffly shrieked. 'It can't be.' She fainted.

'That's torn it!' Lord Toffly agreed. And he fainted too.

'This, on the other hand,' said Rupert Rich, reaching forward gingerly and touching the rubies around Atticus's neck where his head poked out of the velvet cloth, 'may well be genuine.'

Atticus struggled free so that Rupert Rich could take a closer look. He was surprised to see that his fur was nearly back to its normal colour. The dye had rubbed off, just as Mr Tucker had said it would. It felt good being a tabby again, even though his white socks were a bit longer than usual.

'Chaka-chaka-chaka . . .'

'Zip it, you!' Mrs Cheddar raced up. She had found a plaster in first aid. Inspector Cheddar held Jimmy in a wing-lock while she wrapped it firmly around his beak. They threw him in the lobster pot with the other two magpies.

'Where's Countess Von Troutperch?' Rupert Rich demanded.

Michael and Callie picked their way round the netted birds with Mr and Mrs Tucker and climbed on to the stage.

Rupert Rich flashed his teeth. 'Welcome back to this interrupted edition of *Get Rich Quick!*' He beamed at the cameras. 'I'm pleased to say there has been an exciting development. The Tofflys' tiara, as I always suspected, is a cheap fake. It's worth nothing. Zilch. Zero. Zip.'

There was a faint sob from the floor.

'As a result of which, as I understand it, the Tofflys are broke. Bankrupt. Finished!' Rupert Rich grinned at the cameras. 'Tough luck, Tofflys! But never mind because we have a new lucky lady in our midst. Countess Salmonella Von Troutperch, would you please step forward.'

Mrs Tucker took the stage. Everyone clapped.

The duty sergeant rattled his teaspoon against his buttons.

Rupert Rich squinted at the rubies through his eyeglass. 'Countess Von Troutperch,' he announced grandly, 'I can confirm that your ruby necklace is priceless. It's worth trillions. Zillions, I wouldn't be surprised. Congratulations.' He shook hands with Mr and Mrs Tucker and winked at the camera. 'So don't forget, ladies and gentlemen at home, to tune in to *Get Rich Quick!* with me, Rupert Rich, at the same time next week. And remember: *Attack the attic, make a packet!'*

Everyone cheered.

The cameras stopped rolling. Rupert Rich smoothed his hair. 'That,' he said, taking Mrs Cheddar's arm, 'was probably the best show I've ever done. Where did you get those birds from? Absolutely brilliant! Tell me . . . have you ever thought about a career in television?'

Michael and Callie hugged one another in delight.

'Ah, Cheddar,' the Chief Inspector of Bigsworth came up and shook Inspector Cheddar's hand. 'I wanted to congratulate you. You've captured the most criminals I've ever seen in one day. *And* you floored the Tofflys. A brilliant achievement.'

'Thank you, sir.' Inspector Cheddar drew Michael and Callie towards him. 'But I couldn't have done it without these two.'

Callie whispered something in his ear.

'And Atticus, of course!' Inspector Cheddar added.

Finally! It was about time Inspector Cheddar recognised all the work he'd put in. Atticus purred. He lifted his chin so that Callie could give him a tickle.

'Oh, and sir, I think I know where to find the other missing jewellery.' Inspector Cheddar squeezed Michael's hand. Michael squeezed it back. 'The magpies are hoarding it in a nest under the pier.' He glanced down at Atticus. 'My . . . er . . . specially trained police cat led the children straight to it.'

What specially trained police cat? Atticus looked puzzled.

'He means you, Atticus,' Michael whispered.

'He's forgiven you.' Callie grinned.

'Well done, Atticus,' Mrs Cheddar said. 'You were so brave.'

Atticus had never felt so proud in his life. A police cat! He couldn't wait to tell Mimi. He leapt into Inspector Cheddar's arms and started to purr throatily.

Everyone crowded round and made a fuss of him.

'Brilliant work, all of you!' The Chief Inspector of Bigsworth beamed. 'I'll be recommending you and your cat for a position at Scotland Yard, Cheddar. That's it then. Case closed.' He turned to Mr and Mrs Tucker. 'I don't suppose I can interest you in making a donation to the Police Helmets Fund?' he asked casually.

'I'll see if we've got any change to spare,' Mrs Tucker replied. 'After we buy our new house.'

'What new house?' Mr Tucker demanded.

'Toffly Hall of course, Herman.' Mrs Tucker took his arm. 'I've got quite a taste for being the Countess Von Troutperch.'

From the lobster pot, Thug eyed the necklace longingly. ''Ere, Slasher,' he whispered, 'do you think I'd look good in rubies?'

'Gorgeous, Thug, me old prison mate.' Slasher nodded. 'What do you think, Boss?'

'Ah, shut up,' said Jimmy sourly, peeling the plaster off his beak.

25

Early the next morning, when Aisha Rana got back from the Bigsworth Flower Market, a large brown-and-black tabby cat with four white socks and a chewed ear was sitting waiting for her outside the florist in the High Street. Around his neck was a red handkerchief. On the handkerchief was a shiny sticker.

'Wait a minute, you're Atticus!' Aisha bent down to stroke him. 'I saw you yesterday at the antiques fair. You were brilliant! And I've been reading about you in the morning paper! Look!' She held it out to him.

PURR-FECT POLICE CAT PUTS BIRD BURGLARS BEHIND BARS

NEST OF JEWELLERY FOUND BENEATH PIER!

Further down was a picture of Atticus with the Cheddars and another of the magpies being loaded into a police van in cages.

'Not that you can read, of course.' She put the newspaper in the van and brought out armfuls of flowers. 'Inspector Cheddar must be very proud of you!' she said, placing the flowers into a bucket carefully. 'Imagine!' She went back for more. 'A police CAT! Such a clever idea. He told me he trained you himself.'

He did?! Atticus raised a whiskery eyebrow.

209

Aisha finished unloading the van. 'He also said it was *you* who returned my necklace!' She tickled him fondly around the ears. 'Thank you!'

Atticus began to purr. He was pleased Inspector Cheddar hadn't told her it was him who stole it in the first place. But then, after what had happened yesterday, everyone was so happy with him he didn't think it would ever be mentioned again.

Aisha swept her long hair back and grinned. 'Which means you must have met Mimi.'

Atticus's purr grew deeper.

'I thought so!' Aisha laughed. 'She's pretty, isn't she?' She stood up. 'Would you like to take her one?' She gestured to the flowers. 'I'm sure she'd be pleased.'

Atticus raised a paw and pointed to a pretty white daisy with long thin petals and a golden centre which reminded him of Mimi's eyes.

'An aster.' Aisha picked it out of the bucket and trimmed the stem with a pair of scissors. 'She'll like that.' She tucked it carefully into his handkerchief. 'You know the rhyme I suppose – she loves me, she loves me not?'

Atticus blushed.

Aisha laughed at herself. 'What am I saying? Of

210

course you don't! You're a cat! A very clever one, of course . . .' She waved Atticus goodbye. 'Come and see me again, won't you?'

Atticus said meow to thank her and set off at a brisk trot towards the beach.

Mimi was sitting in front of the beach hut gazing out to sea.

'I brought this for you,' Atticus reached up and pulled out the daisy carefully from the handkerchief and laid it down in front of her. 'Aisha gave it to me, actually,' he added quickly. He didn't want Mimi to think he'd stolen it!

'Oh, Atticus!' Mimi sniffed it carefully. 'It's beautiful.' She looked up. 'What's that on your handkerchief?'

'It's my temporary police-cat badge,' Atticus explained proudly. 'Callie found it in her sticker book when we got home from the antiques fair yesterday afternoon. Inspector Cheddar stuck it on. He's going to get me a proper one next week from the Chief Inspector of Bigsworth.'

'Oh, Atticus, that's fantastic!'

'I know!' Atticus glowed. 'And look at this!' He untied the handkerchief. Beneath it was a bright red matching collar. It had a tiny tube fastened on to the buckle with a small metal ring – a bit like the one the messenger pigeon had brought to him in Monte Carlo only two weeks ago. So much had changed since then, Atticus could hardly believe it. 'There's a piece of paper in there,' Atticus explained proudly. 'It's got Inspector and Mrs Cheddar's number on it, in case I get lost. And their address.'

'*Your* address,' Mimi reminded him gently. 'That's where you live now, Atticus. Number 2 Blossom Crescent. That's your home.'

'Yes, I suppose it is, isn't it?' Atticus purred throatily. 'Home.' It was the best word he'd ever heard.

They were silent for a moment, listening to the hiss of the waves.

'Er . . . Mimi,' Atticus said eventually, eyeing the daisy. 'Would you like me to teach you a little rhyme?'

Mimi giggled. 'Okay,' she agreed.

> 'She loves me,
> She loves me not,
> He loves me,
> He loves me not . . .'

And the two of them sat side by side pulling the petals gently from the daisy in the warmth of the morning sun.

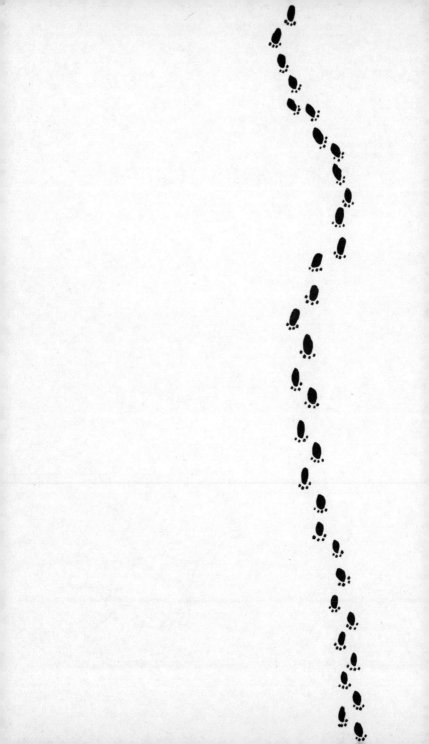

FIND OUT WHAT ELSE ATTICUS
HAS BEEN UP TO . . .

JENNIFER GRAY

ATTICUS
CLAW
Lends a
Paw

'Atticus puts the WOW! into
meow!' Jeremy Strong

COMING SOON . . .
A BRAND NEW SERIES FROM
JENNIFER GRAY, ABOUT
KUNG-FU CHICKENS ON A
TOP-SECRET MISSION!